BARKS, BIKES, AND BODIES!

A TAMSIN KERNICK ENGLISH COZY MYSTERY

BOOK 4

LUCY EMBLEM

This a work of fiction. Names, characters, places, buildings, businesses, products, and incidents are the product of the author's imagination. They bear no relation to actual persons, living or murdered, and every relation to The Malvern Hills, a designated National Landscape in the heart of England. The place is real, but the characters in this book are not, nor are many of the villages you'll visit.

Copyright © 2024 by Beverley Courtney Ltd

All rights reserved.

No portion of this book may be reproduced in any form without written permission from the publisher or author, except for the use of quotations in a book review.

First Edition 2024

Published by Quilisma Books

ALSO BY THE AUTHOR

More mysteries with Quiz, Banjo, and Moonbeam

Sit, Stay, Murder!

Ready, Aim, Woof!

Down Dog!

CHAPTER ONE

"And I know the exact best place for watching the New Year's Eve Fireworks display!"

Tamsin lighted another panel of the gas fire, leant over the tiny terrier on her lap and, pushing her dark hair behind her ear, pointed through the window of her little house in Pippin Lane towards the great mass of the Malvern Hills rising up above the town, a sprinkling of snow visible along the top and the bare sides. The Guardians, as Tamsin always thought of the Hills. Ancient. Permanent. And somehow, wise.

"Thought you might," said Emerald, sitting on the sofa with her long legs tucked under her, her blonde hair draped over Opal's purring head as the cat lay in her favourite place - Emerald's lap. "You probably know every inch of those Hills."

"We've certainly walked many miles along them, haven't we guys?" Quiz lifted her big dark Collie head, saw nothing was happening, gave one muffled thud of her tail on her bed, sighed, and returned her head to her paws.

"It's not so much the 'along them' bit that's hard - it's all the up and down them!" wailed Emerald.

"You're a yoga teacher for Heaven's sake - you should be super-fit."

"I am. But the Hills are still steep," Emerald smiled coyly, "especially those Pixie Steps!"

"They cut off a whole zigzag of the road climbing the side of the Hills, so of course they're steep! But I have to confess, I usually contrive a reason to be in my car when I go up the Hills, so I don't have to walk all the way up."

"*Now* she tells me ..." Emerald affected a grumpy expression, but she couldn't hold it for long before her natural good humour shone through.

"Anyway, the display is at eight on Wednesday. Funny," Tamsin twirled her dark hair thoughtfully with one finger, "I was about to say, 'lucky we have no Wednesday classes', but of course we have no classes at all at the moment!"

"Hence us lounging about here on a Monday evening."

"No Nether Trotley puppy class tonight. And no Cake Stop class for you tomorrow evening either." Tamsin had to raise her voice slightly, as Banjo had started his favourite game of picking up his ball on a rope and dropping it, then catching it on the bounce. This involved plenty of ball-bouncing on the hard floor, and leaping about from the excited blue merle Border Collie, who loved nothing better than playing with his toys.

"It's nice having a break for once in the year. Gets a bit relentless otherwise, week in, week out."

"Yes. A break is very good for us. Everyone else has holidays and time off. Just because we work for ourselves doesn't mean we have to have a slave-master for a boss! It's the season to step back, re-assess. It's the first break we've had since you moved in last year - and I'm so glad for your help with the mortgage, I can tell you: it's made all the difference!" She paused to watch Banjo. "And now is when I do most of my planning - get new ideas for classes, group walks and the like - over Christmas."

"All the same I'll be glad when the money starts to trickle in again," sighed Emerald. "The new Thursday afternoon class at The Cake Stop should help a lot. That's such a great café! Jean-Philippe does so much to help promote my yoga classes."

"I've seen your Thursday posters around the place alright. Got many bookings so far?"

"Enough to get started! It usually grows then by word of mouth."

"That's good! Uh-oh, Banjo - you lost your ball?" The bouncing and jumping had been replaced by puffing and scraping as Banjo lay down, his ears flopping on the floor, and poked under the bookcase to try to reach his errant ball, first with his snuffly nose then with his paw, to no effect. "Moonbeam, help him out would you? Get the ball!"

Tiny Moonbeam jumped off Tamsin's lap, flattened herself like a filleted fish, slithered under the bookcase and scrambled out again trailing the ball - now fluffy with dust - behind her.

"You're showing up my lack of housekeeping, Moonbeam!" laughed Tamsin as Banjo happily reclaimed his ball and started dropping and catching it again. "When do you start? Next week?"

"Yep. I'll be getting bored by next Monday and itching to start classes again! But tell me, what will you do with the dogs for these fireworks? Won't they freak out with all the bangs?"

"Fortunately they care little about fireworks. I got them used to them using videos on the telly when they were puppies. Takes a bit of extra time, but it pays off."

"So they won't mind?"

"I'll be sure to give them a good long walk during the day, then feed them, turn the telly up loud with some soft music, draw the curtains - they'll be right as rain. Even Banjo is ok with fireworks now." She smiled fondly at Banjo, her grey and white collie, his beloved ball between his paws, stretched out asleep now on the hard floor, eschewing the comfy beds all around the place. "Muffin, on the other hand, hates them. So I've given Charity a bit of help in arranging things for her."

"Charity won't be coming out for the display, then?"

"No, 'Seen enough fireworks in my long life, my dear', she told me. She'll keep Muffin company at home and they'll do just fine. Anyway she's visiting her niece near Torquay over New Year, so she may avoid the bangs and crashes altogether. At least being right on the Devon coast, they can only have fireworks on one side!"

"They wouldn't want explosives on boats, I guess!" laughed Emerald, adjusting Opal's position to warm a bit more of her lap. "Oh, how's Muffin doing at your new Dog Tricks Class? I bet she's having fun."

"Loving it! They all are. They're bowled over to see how clever their dogs are. It makes my heart sing to watch."

"Those tricks you do *are* fun! What are you teaching yours at the moment?"

"Moonbeam! You're on!" Tamsin jumped up, tipping her little black and tan terrier on to the floor. Moonbeam stood looking expectantly at Tamsin as she slowly raised her hand with one finger pointing, brought it down towards the dog quickly and said, "Bang!" Moonbeam's eyes lighted up as she threw herself onto the ground on her side and kept totally still ... except for her tail which flipped up and down.

Emerald clapped her hands, helpless with laughter and getting a grumpy look from Opal who had been disturbed from her sleep. "Bang, you're dead! Great idea! Except judging by that tail she's not entirely dead."

"I haven't the heart to stop her wagging her tail," said Tamsin, as she gave the little dog her release signal and delved in her pocket for a treat for her as she sat down again, Moonbeam hopping back onto her lap.

"I bet Chas's boys love that trick."

"I demo-ed several tricks for them at the start, explaining what would suit which dog, and the boys all clamoured at once for Buster to learn that one. It took a while to stop them all running around 'shooting' everyone with their pointed fingers!"

"They're such a lovely family. I get to know them too, what with young Cameron and his mum being in my Monday night class. Who'd have thought such a young child would be so attentive in an adult's class? Fidgety alright, but he really works hard. And he's better at the poses than many of the others."

"More bendy, I guess?"

"Very bendy, and seldom still! Hey, can you turn the fire up a bit - I'm freezing over here!"

"We'll get another 20 pence worth of gas from your new Thursday students," smiled Tamsin, reaching over to turn the knob.

"Exchange is no robbery," quoted Emerald, snuggling Opal closer to her.

"We give a great service, both of us," declared Tamsin. "I'm proud of what I do!"

"And we've earned ourselves this little break. What are you up to tomorrow?"

"I'm going to lie in bed and read! My special holiday activity .."

"*Inactivity*, you mean!"

".. a long walk for the dogs, a bit of a clean-up," she said, pulling a face as she looked round the room at the fluff gathering by the dog beds, "and I'll carry on mapping out my Top Dogs classes for the year, checking the public holidays and all that. It can be a bit of a jigsaw, fitting them in comfortably without breaks in the middle of courses. What about you?"

"I'll be up at the Buddhist Temple in the morning for meditation. Then I can give you a hand with the cleaning when I'm back!"

"Thanks - I'll hold you to that! Hey! How about our last visit of the year to The Cake Stop?"

"We can celebrate a tremendously exciting and successful year .."

"And hope for a quiet and peaceful one starting on Thursday. No more murders, no more Inspector Hawkins hurling accusations about. Just dogs and yoga. It's not a lot to ask."

"Great idea! You're on. We'll head up after we've got bored with housework. About four o'clock?"

"Perfect!" smiled Tamsin happily as she leant back in her chair, luxuriating in just being in her own house, with her dogs, taking time with her friends, taking a break from her precious business, and most of all - looking forward to a drama-free year.

How wrong could a girl be?

CHAPTER TWO

As they clambered up the icy path on Wednesday night, Tamsin and Emerald were glad to have split Tamsin's walking poles between them so they had one each. The sharp points cut into the ice and gave them good purchase on the slippery ground. The path was not too steep lower down the hill, and there was grass either side of it, which was definitely less slippery to walk on. But as they climbed, so the path got steeper and more rocky. The wind, fortunately, was light, and the chill from the snowy ground crept up them from their boots as they breathed in the cold air, huffing out clouds in return. They were glad they'd spent the afternoon filling up with good coffee and delicious cake at Jean-Philippe's cafe.

There was quite a crowd gathering at various vantage points up the hill, a bustle of people jostling for a good position, stamping their feet on the hard frozen ground, clapping their gloved hands together to warm them up. In the raspingly cold night air they were "breathing smoke like dragons" as Tamsin had always said as a child.

Many of the locals were regular walkers, and they were well kitted out for the occasion, in walking boots, warm coats, woolly hats, and quite a few others with poles or old-fashioned wooden walking-sticks. Some had flasks - whether of tea or something stronger, Tamsin couldn't tell - but everyone was happy in anticipation of the display.

"Look, it's Tamsin and Emerald!" a child's voice cried excitedly, and Cameron bounced forward to greet them, followed as ever by his brothers Alex and Joe.

"We're dying to show you what Buster can do!" said Alex, hopping about from foot to foot, waving his arm and just missing hitting Joe in the face.

"Bang!" said Joe, who was used to his brother's jumping about and had ducked in time. "We say Bang! and Buster plays dead!" he demonstrated by half-collapsing, his arms out, eyes closed and tongue lolling.

"I'm dying to see it!" smiled Tamsin. "Where is he tonight?"

"He's at home with Mummy and Amanda," said Cameron.

"She's too young for fireworks," added Alex.

"She's still a baby," said little Joe dismissively.

"That's the best place for Buster to be tonight. Most dogs hate fireworks."

"Yes, Daddy said he shouldn't come," Cameron said with a tinge of disappointment in his voice.

"Daddy's dead right!" Tamsin smiled and nodded at Chas who had joined them to retrieve his boys.

"I read your latest piece in the *Malvern Mercury*," he said. "It was good - I'd never realised that dogs' hearing was so different from ours."

"Of course it is, Dad," said Cameron witheringly. "Buster can hear the mice in the hedge, and we can't."

Chas smiled with pride at his young son, clearly approaching teenage and starting to kick against authority. "You're right, son. And that's why Buster's at home tonight. And always remember," he chuckled as he guided them away, "your mother can hear the grass grow!"

A couple more people greeted either Tamsin or Emerald or both of them, as they carried on up the Hill. Having run classes for years they had many past students - whether for yoga or for dog training, and sometimes both. As was Shirley, whose son they passed next.

Tamsin raised her pole in salute to Shirley's son Mark who she spotted in a small group huddled on a flat grassy patch by the path. He raised his pole and they tapped them together, laughing. "Your Mum here tonight, Mark?"

"No, she's staying home to mind Luke." Tamsin nodded - another dog being looked after, this one a beautiful big white dog - a Great Pyrenees. It made her feel good.

"Where's your special spot?" asked Emerald, giving her yoga student Shirley's son a friendly smile as she trudged past.

"Just up here," puffed Tamsin, as they rounded a wizened tree with two forked wide trunks. "Look - we can lean against the tree so we don't topple over backwards as we say *Ooh* and *Aah!* Glad I've got these thick socks," she added, stamping her feet. "Thank goodness there's no wind tonight or we'd be frozen stiff."

They looked up to the snowy patches on the top of the Hills, sparkling in the moonlight.

"It looks quite ghostly," said Emerald, and shivered.

At that moment they heard a whooshing sound and with a clatter three bikes swooped down the path. Their riders wore dark jumpers with splashes of colour, their helmets with dazzling headlights, peaks, chin-guards, and goggles, completely hiding their faces, giving them the appearance of intergalactic warriors.

Tamsin held her breath as they sped past her tree, then released it with relief as they slowed right down to go past the crowds of people further down the hill.

"Fancy having a meet tonight! They must have known the Hills would be busy," snorted Emerald.

"I guess they usually have the place to themselves. I see their lights on the Hills some nights, but I can't remember if Wednesday is a regular day for them."

"Here come some more!" shouted Emerald, and they sheltered in the safety of their large bare tree as another clump of riders whizzed past, a crunching noise of stones under their wheels as they braked to slow down on seeing the people.

An almighty crash in the sky made them jump and some roosting birds exploded out of the trees in shock - the display had begun!

There were *Oohs*, there were *Aahs*, there was a child crying, there were cries of "Look at that one!" but the overall impression was of crashes and bangs and very loud noise, the smoke from the fireworks drifting across the sky.

It lasted about fifteen minutes, then the people all started chattering amidst applause, their cheeks rosy in the cold, and they began to drift down the path in small groups. The birds who had burst out of the trees at the first explosion were settling back to sleep again. Some of the trail bikers who'd been 'trapped' at the bottom of the hill during the display were heading back up the hill, some stopping to flip up their visors and chat to friends in the crowd, others pressing on - making surprising speed up the steep incline. Being used to the noise of motor vehicles, Tamsin was surprised at how silent they were.

As the smoke of the fireworks cleared away slowly, Tamsin pointed out their house well below them on the side of the hill. "Hot chocolate and the last of the Christmas Cake in front of the fire, I think?"

"Can't wait!" responded Emerald, "but look, the sky has cleared completely - look up at those stars! They look so close - as if you could reach out and touch them." So they delayed and spent a few minutes gazing up at the glittering, sparkling stars, identifying the few that they knew by name - the Plough, Orion, the North Star - before they left their little private viewing area and started their descent, their poles a welcome support as they slipped and slid down the hill.

CHAPTER THREE

"What's that?" said Tamsin sharply as she spotted something metallic glinting in the moonlight down the slope at the side of the path.

"It's a bike!" Emerald had got there first and reached down to touch it, then jumped back with a gasp. "There's someone here! They must have fallen off."

Tamsin stepped past the up-ended bike and saw the sprawled cyclist. "Oh no. Not again."

Emerald turned to look at her, appalled. "You don't think …"

"Look at his neck. That funny angle the helmet is lying at. I don't like the look of this." She felt for a pulse. "Can't feel anything. But maybe I'm feeling in the wrong place. He's not cold. Well, not much colder than my hands. Best ring 999."

With a white face and trembling fingers, Emerald was already on it, and asking for an ambulance. "But we're up the Hills. You can't get an ambulance up here," she was explaining. "And it'll be too dark for a helicopter," she added helplessly. She nodded as she listened to the response, and turned to relay it to Tamsin. "They're alerting Search and Rescue - what's wrong?"

Tamsin was staring at her hand. "I thought I'd see if I could feel a heartbeat ..." she spoke very quietly then held up her hand, which was smeared red.

Both women looked about them hastily, then moved closer together, as Emerald gave the latest information to the emergency person on the phone. She nodded again as she listened. "Ok, we'll move up to a safer spot nearby and wait. We've got our walking poles to defend us!" As they returned to hide behind their tree, Tamsin wailed, "Why does this keep happening to me?"

"Violent accidents? We don't know he's dead yet."

"I'm sure of it now. And unless he managed to impale himself on his brake lever, it doesn't look like an accident either."

They huddled closer, poles up-ended and at the ready, looking about them nervously in the creepy moonlight. The occasional cloud passed over the moon distorting all the shadows and plunging everything into darkness.

"I wish we had a dog here," wailed Emerald.

"I always wish I had a dog here," answered Tamsin, and they settled to wait again.

"Look - there are all the bikes now," Emerald pointed up along the Hills. They could see the lights of the bikers now way up on the North Hill, zigzagging their way up the paths, looking for all the world like a skein of lights on a Christmas tree.

"No-one's noticed him missing."

"No, or they'd be back. Maybe he's new?"

"Maybe he's not one of them."

"Maybe .. why are we whispering?"

Tamsin smiled and stamped her feet, "I do wish I had a dog with me! Where's my hot chocolate?" She reached into her pockets and felt around amongst the dog treats, and found an old fruit bar. "Wonder how long that's been there?" she said as she broke it in half and handed some to Emerald. Their munching eased the tension a little and they relaxed a bit more in their vigil.

It seemed an age - though it was actually less than fifteen minutes - before the Search and Rescue team and their dogs, all of them resplendent in hi-vis outfits, came plodding up the path towards them, and the two friends stepped out to greet them with great relief.

"It's down here!" Tamsin pointed the bike out to the stalwart group of volunteers, and as they offloaded their backpacks and stepped down to see, she busied herself fussing over their beautiful collie. "You're a search dog with nothing to search for, I'm afraid. May I give him a treat?" she asked his handler, who smiled, "May as well make his trip worthwhile," and nodded, "though the boss may want us to search the area in a minute."

"He's dead, alright," called the lead rescuer, bringing the mood right back to earth as he adjusted his head-torch and took the cyclist's pulse - rather more expertly than Tamsin had. "Oh, and what's this?" he said, indicating the red stains on the shirt. "Get the dog to do a square search for a weapon, would you, Pete?" One of his comrades was busy snapping pictures with his phone, from every angle. Another stepped forward and lifted the visor on the rider's helmet. "Know him?" he asked of everyone.

They all shook their heads, including Tamsin - and Emerald, who was now shivering, still clinging to her friend. "We were just up to watch the fireworks," Tamsin told them, "and we're cold!"

"We've called the police, but I can see how cold you are. You'd best leave us your details and get off home. You local? Will they be able to find you?"

"Oh, they'll find me alright!" sighed Tamsin.

The Rescuer looked puzzled, then peered at her face. "Oh I know you! You're that dog trainer woman who keeps finding bodies. You should join us and do it full-time!"

"I think I find quite enough of them on a part-time basis," she gave a crooked smile. "But thanks for letting us go. We won't do a runner. Poor man," she added as she cast a last look in the cyclist's direction, then grasping her pole firmly, set off down the icy hill. She and Emerald looked like a pair of Eighteenth-Century dancers about to start a Gavotte as they held each others' lifted hands to steady themselves and get safely down the icy slope.

Never were they more glad to arrive home and greet their friends, all of whom were cool and calm and not upset by the bangs and crashes of the fireworks earlier on.

And once they were wrapped in blankets in front of the gas fire, mugs of hot chocolate in hand, the Christmas cake weighing heavy in their stomachs, and warm furry bodies snuggled up to them, Tamsin said, "You know, I may take him up on that."

"On what?" Emerald gently stroked the hair between Opal's ears.

"Joining them for Search and Rescue. I think Banjo would love it. He would be working on his own, no need to worry about other dogs. Yes," she smiled, looking up towards the Malvern Hills, their bare snow-covered tops glimmering in the moonlight.

"It'll give you something to fill your evenings, given that your days are pretty full with home visits and classes already?"

"Yes, and I'd get called out for emergencies - fun!"

"Check out your wet weather gear first!" laughed Emerald.

"I'd get one of those groovy orange suits ..."

"Orange? You *never* wear orange!"

"I'd put up with it," Tamsin grinned, "and I think Banjo would look very fetching in an orange jacket." She twirled her finger in her mug and picked up some milky froth to tap onto Quiz's nose. "I guess we may expect a call from our friends at the nick soon enough."

"Tomorrow, I hope. I'm fit for bed, once I've warmed up properly. My toes are still froze."

"Time for you to do some physical jerks!"

Emerald obliged by casting off her blanket and running through a quick sequence of yoga poses that Tamsin could only marvel at: "Hooray for hot chocolate, I say!"

"And hooray for our lovely animals who make the house so warm and welcoming!" added Emerald, her feet softly returning from over her head to the floor.

"Imagine what it would be like without them." Tamsin yawned. "Come on, guys, up to my room," and they all headed to their bedrooms, wondering what the morning would bring.

CHAPTER FOUR

Tamsin didn't have to wait long the next day - she was still on her first coffee - to hear Chief Inspector Hawkins' tired tones over the phone.

"Tell me you had nothing to do with this, Ms Kernick," he said, with resignation.

"Nothing at all. Wrong place, wrong time, that's all there is to it," she replied cheerily.

"Not one of your pupils?"

"Nope. Never seen him before."

"So do you know the local mountain bikers?"

"No." She paused. "Well, yes. I know one or two." She heard the Chief Inspector shifting his position. "Of course. They're all over the place in Malvern. They move here specially so they can go up these steep hills. It seems pain is part of the pleasure." She laughed, "I find getting my pushbike up the hills in town hard enough. I can do without the bone-shaking and flying over bumps."

Inspector Hawkins asked her a few questions about 'the events of the evening', and as he seemed ready to ring off, Tamsin jumped in with "Is that why this fellow crashed? Flying over a bump and impaling himself on his brake lever?" Into the silence she added, "And why is a Chief Inspector interested in a cycling accident?"

"Now you're asking," he responded gloomily. "And you know I can't tell you. But knowing you, you'll find out soon enough. Good day Ms.Kernick," he sighed loudly before ending the call.

Tamsin patted her hand with the phone as she thought hard. At least I know the form now, she said to herself - I have a bit of experience! And she looked at her phone and found her friend the pathologist's number.

"Tamsin!" Maggie answered straight away. "I was wondering when you'd show up! You really have a macabre knack of finding dead people who then end up on my slab," she laughed.

"There I was, off-duty, enjoying the firework display ... Really!"

"I'll believe you, though thousands wouldn't."

"Don't think the good Inspector does. He was hoping I had something to do with it so he could solve the case fast. But tell me - this was no accident, right?"

"No accident. Some kind of spike went into his chest after he'd fallen off his bike. Whether he fell or was pushed is hard to say, but the blow to the head when he landed would have knocked him out."

"Ouch."

"Very ouch."

"Any idea what this spike was?"

"Round with a sharp point - could be some sort of bike tool apparently. Though there's also some bruising around the entry .."

"What sort of bruising?"

"There's part of a round shape that prevented the spike going any further."

"How big is the round shape?"

"Oh, it's .. er .." Maggie flipped some papers, "5.2cm radius. That's a couple of inches, in old money."

"A walking pole! That's pointy with a sort of skirt to stop it sinking into the mud. I have a pair of them."

"Ye-e-es, you could be right. But why would a cyclist have a walking pole?"

"Loads of people had walking poles there last night - there was quite a crowd. I took mine, for a start. Emerald and I used one each."

"Oh Lord, don't tell Hawkins that!"

"They're here, still crusted with mud from previous trips. They're welcome to analyse them. But seriously Maggie - there were lots of walking poles up on the Hills last night. It was icy, the going was slippery."

"I'll have a look - see if I can get an idea of the shape. That could narrow it down."

"You got a name for him?"

"Yes. Don't see why I shouldn't tell you - it's probably in the papers by now. It's .. er .. " Tamsin could hear more papers rustling. "Here! Ferdinand Glossop."

"Ferdinand Glossop? What an unusual name. Where's he from?"

"That I can't help you with. They're on the trail to find out who he was and why he was here. Someone knew!"

"And had it in for him! Or else they're very irascible and didn't like a bike thundering past them. Couldn't have been an accident, could it?"

"You mean he banged into someone who pushed him down the slope then fell on top of him with their pole? Saw what they'd done and scarpered? Unlikely."

"Unlikely. You're right. A real accident would have provoked activity - alarm, calling for help and so on. So someone had a go at him, up there on the Hill .. Must have been very quick."

"And maybe the noise of the fireworks covered it up?"

"You could be right ... Most of the people had gone by the time we came down, and they were below where we found - Ferdinand, was it? You see, I knew a perfect viewing place a bit further up, and Emerald wanted to look at the stars after the display. We must have hung around for a few minutes - five, maybe ten?"

"Sounds as if they're going to have fun finding the perpetrator," said Maggie with not a little glee.

"I s'pose they'll have to interview everyone who was up there .. Hey, why don't we catch up with a walk while we wait to hear more? Orchard near you?"

"Yes, Jez would love to see your gang again. But the orchards are deep with snow over this way. We had an unusually heavy snowfall. Let's go up the Hills this time! You can show me the spot, and your firework viewing platform."

"Done!" and they fixed a date.

"Well, well, well, doggos," said Tamsin when she ended the call and they all looked up expectantly to see if a walk was on offer. "We've got ourselves caught up in another murder!" Moonbeam danced over to her to celebrate .. whatever it was her human had decided to celebrate .. and on a call of "Hup!" she launched herself into Tamsin's arms.

"And you know what this means?" she asked of all the dogs, though it was Quiz who cocked her head, one ear flopped, giving the quizzical look she was named for. "It means we go to The Cake Stop and start a bit of sleuthing!"

Tamsin laughed and whirled around the kitchen, dancing with Moonbeam, with Banjo and Quiz hopping about her legs and dodging her feet. "It may not have been fun for Ferdinand Glossop, but we'll enjoy exercising our brains over this!"

CHAPTER FIVE

The thought was father of the deed, and in no time at all Tamsin had arrived at The Cake Stop, with Quiz the chosen one to accompany her today.

The place was buzzing with people celebrating the New Year's Day holiday, and she had to wait in line to be served, so she amused herself by running Quiz through a few of her tricks. The man in the queue behind her exclaimed with pleasure as Quiz 'sat pretty', her bushy tail sweeping the floor as she wagged with pride. Tamsin smiled demurely, then noticed he was carrying a bike helmet. "Are you a local cyclist?" she asked.

"I am," he smiled proudly, "Well, nearly local. I live on the Hereford road, just past Trumpet. But I'm often over this way."

"You like slogging up hills?"

"Love it!" he enthused, with a dreamy expression.

Tamsin slowly shook her head in wonder. "That's a mystery to me! But each to their own. Hey, did you hear about the accident on Wednesday night? That was a cyclist."

The man shuffled his feet and looked uncomfortable. "Dreadful thing."

"Did you know him?"

"No! No, no. Not one of the usual gang. I hadn't heard of him before. He wasn't in my group that night."

"You were there?"

"Yes, but I was in one of the front groups, so I was on my way to the North Hill before the fireworks even ended."

Tamsin tilted her head, looking like Quiz.

"Ah," he said, "I heard that it happened after the fireworks."

"Not sure. He was certainly *found* after the fireworks finished. But who knows how long he had lain there?"

"Your usual, Tamsin?" they were interrupted by Kylie who had worked through the queue in front of them.

"Yes please, Kylie!" Tamsin nodded a farewell to the guy behind her, noting the wheels turning in his head at the sound of her name.

"You were there!" he said suddenly, his face clearing.

She turned back to him. "I was, yes."

"I heard he'd fallen down a slope, off the path like."

"Yes, he was off the path alright." She looked thoughtful. "Hmm. With the mass of people picking their way gingerly down the icy hill below him, he may not have been noticed, I see what you're getting at."

"Could have happened during the display - plenty of noise to cover it up, with bangs and whistles and oohs and aahs and all that."

"Not to mention bikes swishing past at speed. Don't you guys ever slow down?"

"Oh, I do! I'd hate to run into anyone, or get caught up in a dog lead," he smiled, nodding at Quiz. "Could do some damage - not least to me!" he guffawed.

Tamsin's coffee appeared on the counter and she ended the conversation, gliding swiftly past the cake display, her mouth firmly clamped shut to prevent her drooling and looking a fright. It looked as though The Furies had excelled themselves with mouth-watering cakes for the festive season. The cake-providers were really called Dodds & Co, but were fondly known as The Three Furies as their parents had chosen Classical Greek names for each of them - Penelope, Electra, and Damaris.

Finding her favourite armchair in the window had just been vacated by a previous customer, Tamsin plonked herself into it, put Quiz's mat down beside her, and started to think about what the biker had been saying. "We need to know the time of death, Quizzy-girl," she said quietly. "That's something to prise out of Maggie tomorrow!"

As the coffee shop quietened down a little, Jean-Philippe came over to join her. As the proprietor of the café, he took pride in looking after his customers - which is why he had so many regulars. And unaccountably, he was French.

"*Bonjour Madame la détective!*" he grinned broadly as he sat in the armchair facing her. "*Et bonjour Mademoiselle Quiz!*" He fondled Quiz's ear as she leant in to him.

"Hi Jean-Philippe, what news?"

"It's New Year's Day, the weather is fine, the café is busy ..."

"No, you chump! What news of the murder?"

"It's another murder? *Aïe, aïe, aïe!* You do find 'em!"

"Did you not know? Are they not saying?"

"Nope. All I heard was a cyclist was found dead on the Hills after the fireworks, and that a local dog trainer found him."

"Emerald was there too. We both found him. It was freezing. We had to wait up there for ages in the snow and ice till Search and Rescue arrived. I knew he was dead, though."

Jean-Philippe leant forward, his elbows on his knees. "How?"

"His neck was kinda twisted funny. Then while I was looking for a heartbeat I got blood on my hands."

Jean-Philippe raised one bushy black eyebrow and leant back in his chair.

"I don't know how they find a pulse in the neck on tv murder dramas in a matter of seconds," Tamsin had a puzzled look. "Or rather, they don't. They seem to be able to be sure instantly when they detect no pulse and they turn to their superior and shake their heads sadly. They always do that. I didn't want to touch his neck - I thought it may be broken, and they say not to touch the helmet or anything - so I felt his wrist. And I couldn't find anything, but thought maybe I was doing it wrong. So I put my hand over his heart .." Tamsin made a face, turned away and looked out of the window for a moment, then put her hand on Quiz's head.

"So, what have you found out so far? And don't deny it! I know you are already investigating," his dark eyes twinkled.

Tamsin smiled smugly. "I don't know why I have been singled out by the gods to get involved in murder investigations. But it just seems to happen." She took another swig of her coffee, savoured the taste for a moment, and went on, "Hmm, you don't half make good coffee, Jean-Philippe! He fell or was pushed off his bike, then he was impaled or stabbed. Nasty business."

"*Pas un accident, alors.*"

"Emphatically *pas*."

"And who was he? One of the locals who had a tiff with another biker?"

"His name was Ferdinand Glossop. So far no-one is admitting to knowing him. That guy I was just talking to in the queue is a local mountain biker and he claimed not to know him."

"I thought it was a club who ride up there? So what was he doing in amongst them?"

"Good question. And I'm not sure yet who to ask ..."

Jean-Philippe turned to the counter, saw the queue had temporarily vanished, and beckoned Kylie over. "Kylie rides a bike," he explained. "You're in a club aren't you, Kylie?" he said as she arrived at their table.

"I am. But I don't go up the Hills, if that's what you want to know - I heard the news. I've got a road bike. Do a bit of trekking and the occasional race. But I know quite a lot of them, on-roaders and off-roaders."

"And where do these people all congregate, when they're not here drinking my coffee?"

"There's a bike shop in town where the serious guys all hang out in their lycra."

"There is, yes - of course!" said Tamsin. "That's where I got my second-hand rattletrap when I first came here. But they do super-duper bikes as well. It's now top of my list, thank you Kylie .. Well, not quite the top," she grinned.

"Let me guess, *ton amie la pathologiste?*"

"Too right. Nothing gets past you, Jean-Philippe! I'm getting what I can from her tomorrow - hopefully the time of death if she's prepared to spill the beans."

Jean-Philippe reached across to the next table and picked up the paper which the last customer had been reading. Pointing to the banner he said, "You know who you need to talk to?"

"Feargal! Absolutely, next on my list - hey, talk of the devil! Look who's just over there at the counter!" She waved vigorously and with an answering smile, Feargal casually made his way over to her table, where he put his tray laden with high-calorie iced coffee and a toasted sandwich as well as a massive slice of cake. As Tamsin cursed her stick-thin reporter friend, he pulled up another chair.

And tossing his red curly hair out of his eyes, he said, "Thought I may find you holding court here, Tamsin old thing!"

"Not so much of the old, if you don't mind," Tamsin grimaced.

"The *Malvern Mercury*'s put me on to this - seems I've become their murder reporter. And I knew who to come to first!"

"You'd be right. You won't believe it, but I found *another* body. It really is becoming a depressing habit."

"I'm happy with your corpse-finding habit," Feargal laughed. "Keeps me off the flower shows and Pony Club rallies. Hey this is good cake, Jean-Philippe - oh, he's gone off."

"The queue's got busy again. Kylie suggested the bike shop."

Feargal pushed the plate a little towards Tamsin, his eyebrows raised in question. But steeling herself she said 'No thanks' and sat back smugly.

"*Flying Pedals?*" he asked as he polished off the last of the cake. "I went in there once to get a head-torch. Smells of rubber. Lots of people in lycra comparing spanners."

"That's the one. Fancy a wander over there?"

"Can't right now. Got to see someone in West Malvern." Feargal drained his mug of coffee.

"How have you finished that mountain of food so fast?" asked Tamsin, genuinely amazed.

Feargal shrugged and patted his concave tummy. "Hollow legs," he smiled. And giving Quiz a belated hallo and a bit of crust from his plate, stood up, and said. "Let's go on Saturday. You'll have had time to find out more from Maggie by then." He held up his hands, "Don't deny it! I know how your mind works," he laughed as Tamsin opened her mouth then shut it again with a grin.

It was nice having a friend who really knew you, she thought contentedly, as he walked briskly out of the door, pulling his woolly hat down over his red curls.

CHAPTER SIX

Maggie was waiting with her old black Labrador Jez in the Worcestershire Beacon car park when Tamsin trundled up the slope with her van. She was just cramming her tight black curls into a voluminous fleecy hat. And as Tamsin got out the van carried on wobbling, from all the excitement within, as the dogs were saying, *"We know where we are!"*

They still had to wait and exit the van in an orderly fashion. Not only was it safer that way, but Tamsin knew there was always a chance that as the local dog trainer she was 'on show' and it was important for her own dogs to behave well. It certainly got her enquiries from time to time, from people admiring her dogs' responsiveness.

But with no-one else around, they were able to run over to greet their friends Maggie and Jez before they set off up the Hill. The ground was still frozen and there had been a hard frost the previous night. The trees looked like white lace - there had been no wind, nor yet any sun this morning, to shift the frost off the network of twigs and branches. Looking up they could see the tops of the Hills still covered with a thin layer of snow.

"Lot less snow over this direction," said Maggie after giving Tamsin a quick hug and greeting all the dogs. "Some of our back roads are still blocked."

They started to crunch over the frozen grass. "It tends to get blown off the Hills. And the council grits our road, so I had no trouble getting up here."

"Hmm," said Maggie, "I know what suddenly sparked your interest in seeing me and Jez," she grinned.

"You know I love our walks," smiled Tamsin as they started up the path. "But yes. Curiosity killed the cat. It hasn't killed me yet, and I'm getting a taste for this!"

"I do hope you stay safe. I don't want to find you on my slab one bright morning."

"Do my best. But I feel dragged into this one. I've already had Hawkins on the blower to me."

"I suppose he has to go by the book."

"And the book seems to read 'Page 1: arrest whoever found the body.'"

"Maybe 'suspect' rather than 'arrest'?"

"They carted Charity off, don't you remember?"

"They did too. Though she *was* holding one of the murder weapons," Maggie smiled. "Anyhow, what do you want to know?"

Tamsin paused to catch her breath on the climb, and check she had three dogs still with her. "I'm interested to know when it happened. Have you been able to narrow down the time of death?"

"Not too precisely. By the time he arrived with me, the best I can say is between 8 and 8.30 when you found him. It was so cold that the Search and Rescue guys couldn't help much, either."

"Pity. I suppose it's most likely it happened under cover of all the bangs and shouts."

"And everyone would have been looking towards the fireworks, not realising a murder was taking place so close behind them."

"Gruesome. And, how did he die? I mean it was definitely murder?"

"Yes. He didn't hit a bump and fall off. He was stabbed with something sharp. Probably knocked unconscious by a fall first. Maybe he was pushed over? I've been wondering what the stabbing implement was. Could be a bike tool of some kind - something for prising off tyres? Does that get your wheels turning?" Maggie raised an eyebrow quizzically.

"Haha, very droll ..." Tamsin appreciated her friend's dry humour.

"The head injury would fit with hitting a rock as he fell," Maggie went on. "Could be a ride-by murder. Maybe someone whacked him with a bike padlock and chain as they rode by - though the damage seems to fit more with a flat rock."

"Then they went back and finished him off?"

"Or maybe there were two people unhappy about Mr. Glossop being on the Hills that night."

"Bit far-fetched ... But what about my idea of a walking pole? I brought mine in the van so you can have a look."

"It could well be. I'd like to look at yours. And I'm guessing that different makes of pole have a different pattern on the spike-guard."

"That's true. By the way, they call it a basket. I learnt that when one of mine broke and I had to replace it. I guess that comes from the woven thing they used to have on old ski poles."

"The basket, then. Could be a great help in identifying the pole ... if that's what it is." They'd climbed quite far, and Maggie stopped to look out over the Severn Valley to the East. "Where was the display?"

Tamsin pointed, "Just over there. You see it clearly from up here, and my 'viewing platform' is a bit further up. There were lots of people in this area," she waved her arm as they carried on walking. "And this is where he was, more or less." She indicated a slope at the side of the path. Any police tape that may have been there had now been removed.

They stood, heads bowed for a moment, thinking of what little they knew of Ferdinand Glossop. Which was roughly nothing, as yet. All they knew was that he was no longer. Tamsin gave a big sigh and nodded up the hill.

After a few more minutes climbing they reached the tree, and as they went round it Tamsin showed Maggie the perfect flat space where she and Emerald had enjoyed the fireworks only a couple of days ago.

"I see why you chose this spot!" said Maggie admiringly. "Do you know these Hills inside out?"

"No, not really. I haven't been here long enough - just a blow-in, you know," she laughed, thinking of the many very happy years she had lived under these magnificent Hills. "But I learn new places every time I come up here."

"Is the Worcestershire Beacon your favourite haunt?"

"I first got to know the North Hill - when I was staying at that house on its west flank - you know, when I was house-sitting for the explorer guy. I enjoy the ancient earthworks on the Herefordshire Beacon."

"Bronze Age, aren't they?" Maggie said, craning her neck to look towards the so-called 'British Camp'.

"Yes - nearly three thousand years old. Spooky, really," Tamsin gave a little shiver before continuing, 'There's Pinnacle Hill, which I'll often visit when there are sheep on the other hills - oh, and I have a soft spot for Midsummer Hill. Magical place, that ..."

"So?"

"I like to distribute my walking favours equally!" Tamsin laughed. "But seriously, you could never tire of walking here."

"Don't know about that - I'm tired already from that climb!" laughed Maggie in reply. Maggie was pretty fit, but probably had a few more pounds to lose than Tamsin had. "So, back to the matter in hand - what are you thinking?"

"I'm thinking I need to know an awful lot more about young Ferdinand. What he was doing here, why no-one seems to know him."

"And who disliked him enough to do away with him. Where are you going to start?"

"Flying Pedals!" Tamsin exclaimed.

"Jumping Jehosaphat!" retorted Maggie. "You startled me!"

"It's the bike shop in town," Tamsin laughed brightly at Maggie's quick wit. "Apparently it's a hub for cyclists. Oh dear, I think puns are going to be the order of the day here .."

"Hard to steer clear of them," Maggie grinned.

"Let's 'brake' off," Tamsin groaned, "and go down and look at the poles."

"Right you are," said Maggie, clapping her mitts together with a muffled sound. "It's cold enough up here. Though the dogs are loving it - just look at the speed they can scurry down that icy path."

"They have the benefit of four legs, and lots of claws."

"Four walking poles with multiple spikes!"

They enjoyed watching the dogs plod or scamper, depending on their age and agility, as they descended the Beacon again. Tamsin was brought a few twigs by Banjo and Moonbeam in the hope she'd throw them. "Sorry guys," she said, as she handed the sticks back to them, "remember when Moonbeam nearly sailed over the edge of that quarry? Not taking any chances."

"What's in the quarries?" Maggie asked.

"Some just have very steep drops and a hollowed-out area down the side of the hill, others have filled with water and have a lake at the bottom. So not a good place to fall over."

"Are they not all fenced?" gasped Maggie, her eyes wide.

"They are, but my dogs are too precious. I won't trust their safety to someone else's fence!"

They carried on down the slope. "I used to ride a bike," Tamsin turned to Maggie as they walked, "before I earned enough from Top Dogs to buy the van. Actually, I gave it up because I can't take the dogs when I cycle. And it's really hard work cycling round here!"

"You can't really walk a dog and ride a bike ..."

"Actually, you can, but it's too hilly here for safety, I think. I guess I could carry Moonbeam in the basket!" she laughed, as the diminutive terrier heard her name and waited to see what was required. "Emerald uses my bike now sometimes, till she can get a car. I only know a little about bike tools and maintenance. Just enough to know that someone else would do it much better than me!" she laughed. "So I don't know anything about spiky bike tools."

Loading their dogs back into their respective vehicles, Tamsin first removing some icy snowballs from Banjo's hairy feet - right between the toes where they'd make him sore - they took a closer look at the walking poles.

"See the basket pattern? I'm sure you're right, that these vary a lot." Tamsin pointed to the curved guard above the spike.

"And, of course, that would suggest it was a walker, not a biker who struck the fatal blow."

"Hold your hosses! I propped our poles up against the tree while we watched the fireworks. We only needed them for the icy path. Perhaps people left them lying around, or leaning against the bushes?"

Maggie looked at her as realisation dawned on her. "Anybody. Anybody could have done it!"

"And I intend to find out who!" Tamsin pulled her woolly hat firmly down on her head and folded her arms determinedly. "Tamsin the Malvern Hills Detective is on the case!"

"Let's hope there'll be a thaw soon - in the weather as well as your case! Now I'm going to head home and warm up there. I just have to collect a few things from the office. I'll check over those shapes again."

And so Tamsin had plenty to think about as she waved Maggie and Jez goodbye and drove cautiously back to Pippin Lane for a much-needed warming mug of coffee.

CHAPTER SEVEN

And when she got home she found Emerald, who jumped up saying, "Look at your nose - it's blue! Here let me get you something hot to wrap yourself round," and started making a drink for them both.

"Thanks Em, I'd love that," said Tamsin as she vigorously towelled the wet feathering on Banjo's legs, chest, and magnificent tail. "Let's have a go at your feet too, Quiz .. Moonbeam, you're easy!"

Once the dogs were warm and dry and settled in their beds for a welcome snooze, Tamsin explained to Emerald what she'd been up to that morning. "Doesn't Andrew ride a bike?" she asked, remembering the super-fit sporty young man in Emerald's yoga class who had been involved in the last mystery - actually coming to her rescue on the Hills one day.

"He does, you're right. And I do believe he's one of those nocturnal cyclists up on the Hills. You going to talk to him?"

"You bet," said Tamsin, holding the hot coffee mug in her hands to warm them up as she leaned towards the gas fire, feeling her cheeks redden and prickle as the blood returned to them. "I suppose Linda may know some too, as she shares a house with Andrew?"

"She's pretty gregarious, so that's a fairly safe bet. Can I come?"

"Heck yeah! Love to have you there, with your woo-woo flashes of inspiration," Tamsin grinned at her friend. "Let's drop round there this evening. You don't have a class today? I have my afternoon puppy class starting up again, but nothing tonight."

"Just two private sessions this afternoon. One's out at Halfkey. Thought I'd cycle there, if that's ok with you?"

"Consider it always ok. Does the bike good to be used. It's been a faithful friend and I'd hate for it to feel neglected," Tamsin smiled. "Tell you what, can you find something wrong with it? Then we could go up to *Flying Pedals* on Saturday and have a great excuse to hang around there and find stuff out."

"Ooh, fun! Yes, I'm sure I can find something that I'm too female and helpless to manage."

"Yeah, don't let on how you did a certificate in bike maintenance! Why did you do that, anyway? You never said."

"Oh. Usual reason. Fancied a guy who was into sustainable living. He went everywhere by bike." Emerald shrugged. "He didn't last, but the training did."

"So do you know a sharp bike tool that could have killed our Ferdinand?"

Emerald stroked Opal, as ever on her lap, as she screwed up her eyes and thought. "Some reamers are quite pointy - they're for making precise holes ... do you think that's what did it? Did Maggie say?"

"She thought it could be a bike tool, but we tended towards a walking pole in the end."

"Yuk! What a ghastly thought. Someone really didn't like Ferdinand."

"Let's not think about that right now - time for something to eat before we both go off to work. What'll we have?"

And they fell to deciding what they'd eat for lunch, and when they'd meet again to set off for Andrew and Linda's place. Emerald dropped Linda a text to ask if they were in that evening, and got a delighted reply with lots of smiley faces.

As it happened, it was trying to snow again that evening as they rounded the North Hill to reach the house in West Malvern, causing very slow progress round the bends on the steep slopes of the North Hill. There was a strong westerly wind sweeping the snow in flurries across the road before them, the swirling snow sparkling in the beam of the headlights making it hard to see the way.

"It always looks as though it's coming straight at you," muttered Tamsin as she leaned into the steering wheel trying to make out the road. Arriving safely they found a space to leave the van and didn't have far to go to reach Linda's house, and walked gingerly down the steps to the front door, glad of the hand-rail. Everything in West Malvern was plastered up the side of the hill, so the gardens were all steeply stepped, and from above you could see endless rooves on the hill below.

"How lovely to see you both, my dears!" exclaimed Linda as she opened the front door. "Oh my goodness, more snow! Andrew!" she turned and called, "we have visitors, and I think we'd better sprinkle some more salt on the steps."

Andrew was happy to greet Tamsin and Emerald, "Won't be a jiffy," he said, as he bounded down the stairs like an excited puppy to fetch the salt and sand.

"What's it like with you, on your side?" asked Linda as she led the way to the living room. You'd never guess her age from watching her move, thought Tamsin. Having been a professional ballerina for many years back in the day, she was still both sprightly and graceful, and whenever Tamsin saw her she thought ruefully of the last cake she'd eaten, and resolved - just for a short while - to pay more attention to her diet so that she could stay fit and energetic well into old age.

"It didn't start snowing till we came round the Hills," said Emerald. "But it will probably have reached us by the time we get back. It is beautiful though, isn't it!"

"Pity it's pitch black now," Linda nodded towards their big picture window, its long curtains drawn to keep the heat in. "It looked lovely earlier today, snow all the way across to the Black Mountains."

"Bet they're getting it over in Wales!" said Tamsin. "Hi Andrew!" she added as Andrew strode into the room, swiping his cold hands together to shed the last of the salt.

"That's done," he said in his boyishly cheerful manner. "Won't be riding tomorrow if this lot settles," he brushed some powdery snow off his sleeves and sat down. "To what do we owe the pleasure? Are you on the trail of some dastardly devil again, Tamsin?"

"Yes, I suppose I am! You know the cyclist they found on the Hills on New Year's Eve? Well, it wasn't 'they', it was 'we'. Emerald and I found him."

"Ooh, nasty!" said Linda with feeling.

"It was. Very nasty," Emerald nodded slowly. "And of course it's twitched Tamsin's detecting nerve."

"So you're on the trail, Tamsin?" asked Andrew, trying hard to contain his energy and sit still.

"That's right! And as he was a cyclist, all in the usual biking gear, I thought you may have some ideas. You're into night-riding, aren't you?"

"I am. I don't go every week, but I do enjoy a whiz round the Hills in the dark - it's exhilarating, you know!"

"Each to their own ..." shrugged Tamsin with an answering smile from Linda.

"I suppose you go at night so you have the place to yourselves?" asked Emerald.

"That's why, yes. We can really let rip."

"And were you there on New Year's Eve?"

"No. Linda's sister was visiting that night, with her son, and I stayed home for dinner instead."

Tamsin and Emerald smiled warmly at Linda, who said, "Don't see her very often, so it was a special visit."

"And I knew it would be busy anyway, what with the fireworks going on," Andrew added.

"So do you belong to a club? Or do you just gather together on an *ad hoc* basis?"

"There are some hardcore bikers who are there every week. They tend to hang out at *Flying Pedals* - know the place?"

"Yes, I do! That's where I got my road bike from when I first came here. Sort of bicycle shop cum social club, isn't it?"

"Yeah, that's it. People hang around there drinking tea for hours while they fiddle about with bits of bike. It's good for business though, they'll often end up buying the latest kit or a new lid."

"Translation please, Andrew," Linda said quietly.

"Ah sorry! A lid is a full-face helmet, you know, with a brim and a chin-guard - serious stuff. The kit is what they wear - special trousers, performance jerseys, armour ..."

"Armour?!"

"Body protection - like elbow pads. Some people wear full torso armour."

"Ferdinand should have been wearing that," Emerald said sadly.

"Really? How would that help? Didn't he fall off and bang his head?"

"Worse than that," Tamsin decided to spill the beans to her friends. "He fell off, or was knocked off, and possibly lost consciousness. But he died because he was stabbed, in the chest."

"Oh my!" gasped Linda.

"I thought it was an accident!" said Andrew, with a look of horror.

"It was not." Tamsin leant forward, elbows on her knees. "I don't know why anyone wanted to kill Ferdinand Glossop, but .. I'm not having it!"

There was a stunned silence. Then Andrew spoke. "Ferdinand Glossop. Ferdie? I seem to remember hearing about him at *Flying Pedals*. Apparently he was asking a lot of questions."

"Did you meet him there?"

Andrew blushed to his sandy ginger roots. "I, er, heard about it."

"Who from?" Tamsin was fascinated by his discomfiture.

"Um, I think it was Sara," he said, most unconvincingly. "Yes, pretty sure it was Sara," he nodded, vigorously.

The three women all smiled to themselves. Tamsin had first met young Sara in the Bishop's Green affair. Then she popped up again in Emerald's yoga class, the one where Emerald also lost a student. Yoga classes were one of Andrew's many forms of exercise, and he had clearly been very taken with her.

Emerald piped up, "So what was Sara doing in *Flying Pedals*? I'd have expected rather to find her in 'Flying Hooves'," she grinned.

"Oh! Er .. she does some Saturday work there. Earning herself enough to enter shows with Crystal - the one with the hooves!"

"That's handy! I didn't know she was interested in bicycles."

"Oh yes, she cycles across from home. She's jolly fit, you know," Andrew's face shone.

"I'd love to see Sara again!" said Tamsin. "It's Saturday tomorrow - I think a visit to *Flying Pedals* is indicated," she smiled knowingly at Emerald. "Thanks, Andrew - that's a real help!"

Linda twitched the heavy curtain aside and peered out. "I don't want to hurry you two, but this is beginning to settle. I think you may want to get back before the roads get bad."

Tamsin and Emerald jumped up gratefully and made their goodbyes. They had learnt a lot!

"We've got a lead now," hissed Tamsin as they picked their way up the steep steps.

"This is getting fun!" Emerald replied from a couple of steps below her, brushing some snowflakes from her eyelashes. "I wonder what tomorrow will bring ..."

CHAPTER EIGHT

When tomorrow came, they were keen to get over to *Flying Pedals*. The sky had cleared, the dense early morning mist having lifted to reveal the mighty Malverns towering over them, and there was a pale wintry sun doing its best to melt the thin coating of snow, leaving stripes of dull green where it had done its work, and on the roads it was helped greatly by the gritting lorries that had been out during the night making the roads safe.

"It's beautiful!" said Tamsin, nodding to the part of the Hills they could see from the kitchen window. She was first to reach the kettle today and therefore had the honour of feeding Opal who, unlike the dogs, would not stand for any delay in her food being served. "I feed you in self-defence," snorted Tamsin, "so that you stop that dreadful wailing!"

Emerald smiled, "It is lovely, yes! Let's *walk* to the bike shop instead of loading the bike in your van. Who will we bring?"

"I think Moonbeam is the easiest to manage in a cluttered shop, and she'll fit in the bike basket too!"

So they set off in a while, pausing as they walked to admire the hard frost on the tracery of the trees, now melting and dripping on their south-east sides. They glanced up the hill towards the Beacon, stopped for a moment - but neither felt the need to speak.

They were breathing clouds of mist as they arrived up the steep hill at the little bike shop - a ramshackle building set into the side of the Hills, looking as if it had grown from the hillside and been built out of found materials by gnomes and woodland creatures. But inside was another world!

As they pushed open the heavy steel door a strong smell of rubber and oil greeted their noses, Moonbeam's nostrils twitching at the strange new smells. There were bikes everywhere. Lined up in smart rows, hanging from the walls, dangling from the ceiling. And the impression of hard shiny metal throughout was softened by the rows of brightly-coloured helmets and the racks of dayglow clothing. Some were made to cover most of the body, and others - the clingy lycra numbers - as skimpy as was possible. Most were designed to be seen clearly on the road, though there were some black and dark blue racing suits for off-road.

Tamsin pulled off her woolly gloves and fingered the tiny garments carefully, thinking of all the cake she'd have to do without in order to fit them. She shook her head sadly as she looked up to see who else was in the shop.

Up at the desk was a jolly, round woman in her fifties, chatting cheerily to a customer deliberating over lighting options for his helmet. Aha, thought Tamsin - a night-biker!

"You need to be sure to see and be seen off-road - specially these days," the cyclist said with a knowing look as he fingered the lights and gave the shop assistant a wink.

"Ooh, isn't it awful!" responded the lady dutifully. "Were you there?"

"I was, but miles away at the time," he replied airily. "What about you?"

"Oh, we were in Oxford, bringing in the New Year with family, you know."

Tamsin picked up Moonbeam and moved towards the bikes to affect interest in them but just to be sure she didn't miss anything.

"They say he was new to the area," he continued. "Did you know him?"

"He was in here last week - asking loads of questions .."

The cyclist looked up sharply. "What kind of questions?"

"Brenda!" called a man's voice sharply from the room beyond the counter, "Here a minute."

Brenda went into the back office from where Tamsin could hear mutterings. It sounded as if the man wanted her to keep her counsel. Only he didn't put it as politely as that.

"Ok, Howard, whatever you say," she said huffily as she emerged again. "Which light would you like, Johnny?" she asked the customer, folding her arms to indicate that the interesting subject was closed, and re-applying her smile.

He settled on the one he wanted and completed his purchase, looking around the shop as Brenda packed his lights. Tamsin studied the gears on a pink bike very carefully. Johnny pocketed his lights, frowned at Tamsin, saw Emerald still holding her bike near the door and headed straight for her.

"Having trouble with your bike?" he asked.

Emerald gave one of her ravishing smiles, looked as girly and helpless as possible, and said, "Are you one of the mechanics here?"

"I'm not, but I'm always ready to help a damsel in distress," he leered, stroking her bike's handlebars.

Tamsin, watching this, called out, "Hey Em, they're free now!"

As Emerald pushed her bike towards the counter, Johnny called out, "Bye Emma, see you around ... I hope!" and left the shop.

"Not if I see you first," Emerald said under her breath, and "Who was that?" loudly to Brenda.

Brenda grinned, "Now that .. was Johnny Lightholder," she said, loading the words with meaning. "Fancies himself rather, with the ladies, know what I mean?" Emerald cast her eyes upward.

"He was interested in that awful case of the man who died on the Hills?" asked Tamsin.

Brenda glanced over her shoulder at the back room, then leant forward over the counter and said quietly, "I sort of got the impression he knew him. Fishing, you know? For information."

"*Fascinating!*" said Tamsin warmly and encouragingly. And Emerald nodded vigorously to spur Brenda on.

Brenda didn't need much encouragement, and clearly loved nothing better than an audience. "You see, that poor Glossop man was in here last week," she nodded vigorously, both chins wobbling as she did. "He was trying to track someone down."

"Who?!" chorused Tamsin and Emerald, and Moonbeam - now perched in Emerald's bicycle basket - cocked her head with interest to hear the answer.

"Well he was just enquiring about when the Nighthawks meet on the Hills - that's the group that ride there." She glanced over her shoulder again and lowered her voice. "I got the impression he didn't know *who* he was looking for, but would know when he found them, you know?"

"I wonder what he was after?" said Tamsin.

"Whatever it was it seems to have got him killed ..." added Emerald.

"Could it have been something wrong in the Nighthawks? Like performance-enhancing drugs?"

"That would only matter if they were racing in an event," Brenda said thoughtfully, "but a lot of them do!"

"It's serious stuff, then?" asked Tamsin, to which Brenda nodded knowingly, "Oh yes, very serious they are about their racing."

"Hmm," added Emerald, "What about match-fixing then? Do people bet on the outcomes?"

"People will bet on anything," snorted Tamsin, who had always viewed gambling as one of the dark arts.

"Could be, I suppose," said Brenda doubtfully, as a stern voice came from the office, followed by its stern-looking owner, "Can we do anything for you ladies?" asked Howard.

"Oh, yes please," Emerald turned on the helpless look again, keen to rescue their informant from this grumpy man. "There's something wrong with the chain - it keeps jumping. Nearly had me off yesterday going down Church Street!"

"Right then," he turned back to the office and bellowed, "Sara! Fetch up Jason, would you?"

There was a banging of doors, and a lean young man with spiky black hair and oil-stained tattooed hands ambled in.

"Jason, when can you fix this bike chain for the lady?"

Jason wiped his nose on his sleeve, peered at the bike, poked at the chain, stepped back and pronounced, "Monday."

"Oh, I was hoping it could be today! I need it on Monday to get to work," Emerald's eyelashes were doing overtime.

"What's Mark doing? Could he take a look?"

"Yeah, Mark could do it. You asked when *I* could do it, Dad." Jason folded his arms and glowered at his father.

"Take it back to the workshop and have Mark fix it," Howard glowered back. The fizzing tension between father and son was palpable. Jason and his mother exchanged glances.

"Would I be able to collect it today? Or will we wait?" More simpering from Emerald, surprised that it didn't seem to be working on the younger of the two men.

Brenda cut in, "Can you do a bit of shopping and come back in an hour or two? I'm sure Mark will have it ready by then!"

Emerald smiled her thanks, handed the bike to Jason while Tamsin hurriedly snatched Moonbeam out of the basket, and they were about to leave when a slim dark girl emerged from the office saying, "Ok if I take my lunch-break now, Brenda?"

"Sara!" cried Tamsin, "How lovely to see you! I had no idea you worked here." The lie was for Brenda's benefit. Sometimes Tamsin worried about her ease in being able to tell whoppers, but she felt that in pursuit of the truth it was just about forgivable.

Sara was pleased to see her friends and shepherded them out of the shop. When they reached the pavement outside she said, "I've got an hour - let's go to The Cake Stop while you wait for the bike to be fixed. I was listening to you talking to Brenda, and I have to say I wasn't a bit surprised at you taking an interest in a *murder*! I think I may be able to help you ..."

CHAPTER NINE

The three women chattered happily as they walked to Jean-Philippe's.

"So how long have you worked at *Flying Pedals*?" asked Tamsin, "I had no idea till Andrew mentioned it!"

"Only a couple of months, just on Saturdays usually, though I'm doing a few extra days while I'm on holiday from College. I cycle across from Bishop's Green - it's quite a nice run, as long as the weather's good! I need some extra dough to pay Crystal's entry fees for shows. Dad foots all the other bills, but insists I earn money for such 'fripperies'!" she laughed.

"That's handy," said Emerald.

"Yeah, and I get to visit these lovely shops too, in my lunch-break. There are some really quirky shops here - but of course you know that already, living here! They're all closed by the time I come to your yoga class on Tuesdays with Julia, Emerald, and of course I can only come to that in the holidays."

"So how did you get here today? You hardly cycled in the snow!"

"Dad had Rory drive me over in the Land Rover - you remember Rory Jackson, his factotum round the estate?"

Tamsin and Emerald nodded as they remembered the part Jackson had played in the affair at Bishop's Green. "He's settled in again, then?"

"He has, yes," said Sara quietly.

Once seated with their coffees and cake - "My treat!" said Tamsin expansively - and Jean-Philippe and Kylie had both made a fuss of Moonbeam, Tamsin said, "Now just what did you mean, Sara? How can you help us?"

"Andrew said you knew something about this Glossop character," added Emerald.

"Well," said the fit, slim, Sara, as she ladled sugar into her coffee, causing Tamsin to rail against the gods at how people's metabolisms had been handed out, "Well, he was hanging around the shop asking questions."

"We heard that!" said Tamsin impatiently, "what questions?"

"He was clearly trying to track someone down, but didn't know their name. Just that they raced at night on the Malverns. Brenda was all agog, as you can imagine, dying to know what he wanted. But he just clammed up when she tried to find out."

Tamsin gave Moonbeam, on her lap, a morsel of her raspberry sponge cake. "So what did she tell him?"

"There wasn't too much she could tell. But she gave him a flyer for the Nighthawks: it lists some names and contact numbers. And she scribbled the club secretary's name on the back. He was delighted with it. I remember he waved the paper about and said, '*got it!*'"

"So one of the names on the paper, or the club secretary's name, was who he was looking for!"

"Maybe. Or maybe it just gave him names of more people he could talk to. Anyway, he clearly decided to beard them in their den, and went up to join the ride on Wednesday night."

"Can anyone join in?" asked Emerald. "You don't have to announce yourself, or sign up, or something?"

"I think you're meant to. But it was dark. No-one would notice another biker, decked out in the same gear."

"You're right." They all sipped their coffees thoughtfully.

"They call them 'poachers', people who gatecrash a ride without paying."

"Must happen quite a bit then, if they have a name for it," said Emerald.

"I suppose so. But it's fair enough really - it takes a lot of work to establish a club and its rides."

"We wondered .." said Tamsin, "you see, this is different from the other murders we've been involved with .."

"What a weird thing to say!" giggled Sara.

"Pretty weird, you're right! But it's different because we don't know anyone involved. We're not in the mountain biking crowd."

"We *thought* we didn't know anyone involved," Emerald corrected her. "But look who we've met already! Andrew does a bit of it, Sara's in the bike shop .."

"And there's someone else you know too," smiled Sara mysteriously, leaning back from the table and folding her arms.

Tamsin and Emerald looked at her expectantly.

"The one who's fixing your bike right now - Mark."

"Mark?" Emerald tilted her head.

"Not ... Mark Bendick?" Tamsin raised her eyebrows.

"The same." Sara smiled smugly.

"Shirley's troublesome son?" asked Emerald.

"Yep, the one we keep running into in our, er, investigations. How did you know we knew him, Sara?"

"Shirley comes to yoga, remember?"

"Of course! Oh yes, I remember he was doing some kind of mechanic's course to keep him on the up and up. Thought it was motorbikes he was into?"

"Seems he needs to do some work with push-bikes too, to finish his program," Sara explained. "Actually he's got quite involved. He's keen on cycling himself - he's got a smart road bike already and he got himself a new mountain bike so he could join the Nighthawks. He's showing a flair for organising, and - being at the shop - he's doing some of their planning for them."

"The plot thickens!" giggled Tamsin with renewed enthusiasm. "If Mark's around there's probably trouble lurking. He's a bit of a trouble-magnet, as well as driving his poor mother demented as she tries to cover up for him and bail him out."

"I bet she's happier he's cycling instead of motor-biking now," said Emerald, thinking of Shirley.

"Well, cycling can be dangerous too, you know," Sara replied.

"You're telling me!" Tamsin drew down the corners of her mouth. "Anyhow, we wondered whether this Glossop guy was investigating performance-enhancing drug-taking, or match-fixing, or something like that."

"Hmm, could be ..." Sara put down her coffee mug. "Hey, perhaps he was a journalist!"

"Ooh, you know who could find that out for us!" said Emerald excitedly.

"Yes, and he should have been here. We were meant to be meeting up at the bike shop."

"That's funny. Feargal usually texts if he's held up." Emerald looked concerned.

Tamsin pulled out her phone. "No. Nothing ... Oh hang on! I hadn't switched it off airplane when I got up today. Duh! What an eejit I am ..." She tapped the screen a few times and said, "Ah, here we are. Yes. Poor Feargal *had* sent a text. Let's see." She read aloud.

Sorry can't get away this morning. Can we meet later on? At J-P's perhaps?

She tapped a quick reply and rubbed the blushes from her cheeks. In no time the phone buzzed and was swiftly followed by Feargal pushing the big café door open and looking round for them.

"I'm so sorry!" Tamsin was effusive in her apologies. "Let me get you a coffee. Let me see, large Cappuccino with half a pound of sugar, right?"

"You got it! And order a toasted sambo too, please," laughed Feargal as he patted Moonbeam and smiled softly at Emerald, who was saying, "You remember Sara, don't you? From Bishop's Green?"

"Of course," he grinned as he drew up a chair. "Hallo again! You not doing something horsey this weekend?"

"I will be tomorrow. Crystal's at home for the Christmas break. But on Saturdays I work in *Flying Pedals* now, to save money for my entry fees later in the year."

"Aha!" Feargal clasped his hands together in front of him, "so Tamsin is grilling you for info on our unfortunate victim?"

"I offered to help," said Sara, with a little pout.

"And you have been really helpful!" added Tamsin, placing a brimming mug before Feargal and pushing the sugar over to him. "Kylie's bringing over your toastie in a minute. Looks as though you need it, your cheeks are blue and your nose is red."

"You say the sweetest things, old girl," smiled Feargal. "I was trying to get in touch with someone for a piece we're doing on grubby councillors. He's proving very elusive. Lots of tramping about and no show. At least the pavements are clear now, the ice has gone except in the very shaded bits."

"Oh, I have something else," Sara jumped forward, "I nearly forgot! The Nighthawks are having a little memorial for Ferdinand up at the spot he died. It's tomorrow afternoon - um - at 2 o'clock. I won't be there - I'll be spending the day at home with Mum and Dad once I'm back from my ride."

"Ooh thanks, Sara - fascinating! Don't worry - we'll definitely be there!"

"So Crystal's home for the holiday?" asked Emerald, nodding to Tamsin at the same time.

"Yes, she stays at college during the term - couldn't be boxing her back and forth every weekend. So I'm making the most of our lovely rides around home over the Christmas break."

"Here you go, Feargal," Kylie cleared a space on the table, giving it a quick wipe with her ubiquitous tea-towel, and put the toasted sandwich there.

Feargal grabbed it with both hands, smiled his thanks to Kylie and Tamsin and just before taking his first huge mouthful, said, "Ok, what's the story so far, then?"

Tamsin outlined the events of the morning as Feargal chomped and chewed, with Sara and Emerald both chipping in with points they thought important.

"May we assume that competitive mountain biking, like any other sport, is rife with hostilities, jealousies, macho posturing, and people who will do anything to win?" asked Feargal as he gave his last crumbs to an expectant and grateful Moonbeam and started on his coffee.

"I get that feeling," said Tamsin.

"Me too," Emerald shuddered at the thought of Johnny Lightholder's advances.

"I see a lot of it in the shop," said Sara. "They want to wear what the successful guys are wearing, and they're always sniffing about for information."

"'Guys'," said Feargal. "No 'Gals'?"

"There are a few, but they seem much more low-key about it all."

"Do they ride with the Nighthawks too?" asked Emerald.

"They do, but the women have separate competitions. There aren't that many women bikers in this group, I believe, so perhaps they stick together more. Probably have enough to put up with from the blokes!"

"So the blokes are pretty hard-core?"

"They certainly like to appear so!" laughed Sara. "They love the danger of what they do - flying about at speed through trees and rocks."

"Very alpha male," murmured Tamsin, and Emerald shuddered again.

"But they're very good at it all the same," added Sara. "Great Britain always does very well at the World Championships. Nighthawks is a serious group - they had people in the Worlds previously, and they're keen to get in again."

"And you say our chum Mark has re-appeared, and in his attempts to follow his mother's bidding and keep to the strait and narrow, he's bang in the middle of another mystery," observed Feargal, tossing his floppy auburn hair off his forehead as he licked his buttery fingers.

Watching this, Tamsin said, "Mark has sticky fingers when it comes to crime. We'll need to have a chat with him," and Emerald added, "Best not let Shirley know - she does worry so."

"True. Though she's not barmy. If there's been a murder to do with bikes and her son is working in the bike shop ..."

"She may put two and two together."

There was a pause while they thought about the harassed mother and her errant son, and their involvement in both the Nether Trotley mystery where they first met, then again in the yoga class murder.

"Hey Feargal," Tamsin blurted out. "What's the news from the police? Where are they at in this?"

"Wondered when you'd ask that! It seems they're struggling a bit. They're interviewing all the cyclists of course, but they're not coming up with anything of interest. No leads at all at the moment."

"It was definitely murder, not an accident?" said Sara quietly.

"'Fraid so. He was stabbed with something. Forensics are doing tests to establish what it may have been. I know you had an idea it was a walking pole, Tamsin."

"Definitely. Sure of it. Though I've no idea if there's a bike tool that could leave a similar mark. What do you say, Sara - any tools in the bike shop that have a point and a round skirt, like a walking pole does?"

Sara thought for a moment. "There are a few pointy things, but I don't think any have a round bit on them too. I can have a snoop round the workshop."

Feargal leant forward, elbows on knees. "You know, if this is to do with match-fixing, or performance drugs, there'll be a lot of money wrapped up in it. I really think you should take care. If that's what got young Ferdinand topped, then they won't hesitate to despatch anyone poking their nose in."

"Can you do your snooping when you're taking a cup of tea in to them? Or chat to Mark while he's working? Don't be too obvious, Sara," said Tamsin, nodding to Feargal. "You're right, Feargal. It could be dodgy. I want to talk to Mark, and I think we should infiltrate the Nighthawks. You any good on a bike, Feargal?"

"Thought you'd never ask this fine figure of a man! I can scoot about on the Hills a bit, but not any of the really hard stuff."

"What about Andrew?" piped up Emerald. "He said he goes up there sometimes. You remember Andrew, Feargal, who rescued Tamsin from marauders up on the Hills that time?"

"I do. Nice chap. Into anything athletic. Red hair - what more can I say?" Feargal swept his red curls off his brow with a flourish and a grin. "Want to give me his number, or will you ask him, Tamsin?"

"I'll do it. I'll have him ring you for a chat. I definitely think this is the way to go. We have to know who the main players are in the group and what the dynamic is. We've got a good chance of doing just that tomorrow, at the memorial. Only then can we find out who Ferdinand was looking for and - perhaps - why."

CHAPTER TEN

They all walked back together to *Flying Pedals* after their lunch break, and were glad to see the sun - although weak - had almost cleared the pavements of snow and ice so they didn't have to cling to each other to stay upright.

The bell trilled as they pushed through the main door and saw Mark standing at the front desk, Tamsin's bike propped up against it.

"Brenda gone for lunch, Mark?" asked Sara as she peeled off her coat and gloves and approached the desk.

"Yeah. And Harold wanted to talk to Jase about something, so they've left me holding the fort."

"You're ok, you can bolt back to the workshop now I'm back! But, you remember Tamsin and Emerald, don't you? And Feargal from the *Malvern Mercury*?"

"Blimey." Mark swallowed hard, clearly remembering only too well. "This your bike, then?"

"Yes!" Emerald stepped forward with a beaming smile. "Have you fixed it for me?"

"Well I checked everything. Couldn't find why the chain jumped on you. I've tensioned it all correctly, oiled it, of course. And while I was about it I checked the brakes and the handlebar tracking. Nice little bike. Shouldn't give you any trouble now." He patted the handlebars fondly.

"Oh thank you! That's wonderful! How much do we owe you?"

"I'll let Sara deal with that," said Mark, about to leave them.

"Hang on a minute, Mark - I think you could really help us." Tamsin leaned towards him. He turned, looking like a rabbit in the headlights, and gulped again. "Sara was telling us how brilliant you are at this mechanicking thing. I'm impressed by how well you're doing, really," she smiled disarmingly at him. And, duly disarmed, he turned round to her, and blushed as he looked at the floor. "Are you really?"

"I am. And I bet your Mum's proud of you too."

That seemed to seal it. Mark shuffled and said, "What do you want to know?"

"I gather you're an important part of the Nighthawks organisation." Mark beamed shyly. "It's this guy, Ferdinand," she went on. "So did you know him at all?"

Mark shifted from one foot to the other.

"You're not in trouble, Mark! It's just that ... you see, Emerald and I found him - his body - and I - *we* - feel that we want to know more about him. How he came to be there, who he was trying to track down ..."

"And who killed him," added Feargal bluntly.

Tamsin scowled at this interruption of her carefully soothing words. "That too. Of course."

Mark shifted his weight from one foot to the other again and fingered the bike handlebars. Bikes he could understand and manage. People not so much. "I got no idea who done him in," he blurted out. "He seemed a nice enough guy. He was asking Brenda all about the Nighthawks. See, I was getting some parts from the front of the shop when he was here. And Howard came out of the office and interrupted them. So Brenda scribbled something on a Nighthawks flyer and he scarpered, waving it."

"Howard didn't want Brenda to answer his questions? That's interesting ..."

"There's nothing Brenda likes better than a good ole chinwag, so perhaps Howard wanted her to get on."

"Sure." Tamsin said, understanding him precisely. " I know you're an observant fellow, Mark. You didn't happen to notice what he was asking, did you?"

"Not really. He was trying to find someone, but wasn't sure of their name. He kept saying Ambrose something, but it didn't ring any bells with any of us."

"And he thought this Ambrose was a Nighthawk?"

"A mountain biker, he said."

"Ambrose ..." said Sara thoughtfully. "I'm going to have a quick look in the records," she added quietly, turning on her heel and firing up the computer. "Not a common name," she muttered as she tapped the keyboard. "Hmm, it's all listed in surname order ..."

"That name's found more in Ireland," said Feargal, now leaning over her shoulder in the office. "Try looking for Irish surnames."

Emerald turned to Mark, "Did you get the impression that Ambrose was a personal friend of Ferdinand's? Or did it sound more like a business deal?"

"Good question, Em," whispered Tamsin.

"That's very hard to say." Mark shrugged his shoulders, screwed up his eyes, and thought hard, like a small child trying to remember his times tables. "I think you're on to something there. Yes, I think it sounded more a personal thing. There was something about the way he asked - Oh, here's Howard back," he added as he saw some figures walking past the shop window.

"Feargal!" barked Tamsin, to Moonbeam's surprise.

"Go to the invoice page," he hissed to Sara, as he emerged from the office saying loudly, "Your funny surname's messing up the system, Tamsin! Sara couldn't spell it. So that's all fixed, Mark, thank you. Got your card, Tamsin?"

"Hello my dear," said Brenda as she bustled in, tossing her coat onto a hook just inside the office and presenting herself, complete with beaming smile, in her usual position at the desk. Howard had gone straight to the office and stayed there, out of sight. "Got everything sorted? Bike ok now?" She smiled expansively, for all the world like a baker showing off her scones fresh from the oven.

Everyone joined in with the smiles as Mark slipped away and Sara finally managed to print the invoice, handing it to Brenda with a flourish and a laugh. "Never could spell well - sorry!"

"Here's my bank card, Brenda - thank you so much for doing it so quickly. Here Moonbeam, you can have another ride!" Tamsin lifted the little black and tan terrier into the basket as Emerald swung the bike round towards the shop door - not easy amid the rows of shiny new bikes and dangling clothing - Feargal following her.

Brenda tilted her head and produced another double-chin as she said, "Oh, that's so cute! The little dog in the basket ... aww."

"Lovely to see you again, Sara!" said Tamsin as she took back her card and receipt and turned to follow her friends out of the shop.

Once they'd got a little away from the building Feargal said quietly, "That was close! Think he suspected anything?"

"Howard? Don't think so. He disappeared straight into the office. Hope Sara knows how to delete her history ... "

"She looked pretty smart about it," said Feargal. "So what do we all think?"

"I think .. we shouldn't be discussing this in the street. Let's go up this path into the Hills a little way." As they climbed into the woodland, Tamsin released Moonbeam from the basket and watched her little dog scurrying around, nose to the ground.

"Did you see the prices on those bikes, by the way?" asked Tamsin. "Nearly ten grand!"

"No wonder they have steel doors on the shop," said Emerald. "I had no idea bikes cost so much, and there are dozens there!"

"So there's clearly money at stake in all this," said Feargal pensively. "So where are we? Sara will see what she can find in the records about Ambrose - perhaps she'll ring you, Tamsin, when she's off work tonight?

And I'll do some sniffing in the *Mercury* archives, see if he's a mountain biker, or anything else I can find."

Emerald propped the bike against a tree. "Mark was very touched by what you said to him. He does seem to have turned over a new leaf. Hopefully the leaf will stay the right way up now." Emerald was a great one for mixing her metaphors.

"I think you'll find that the leaf is a page in a book, rather than the green thing on a tree, Emerald," the pedantic Tamsin said, then seeing Emerald's discomfiture added, "I could never understand why you'd want to invert a leaf on a tree, till it dawned on me one day ..." and she smiled reassuringly.

"Maybe Mark will be able to give us more information when we need it. He did seem willing." Feargal brought the conversation back on track.

"Wonder if he'll go to the memorial?"

"Hmm, I wonder. Can't wait to see who turns up tomorrow. It seems decent of them to honour poor Ferdinand, specially as no-one seems to have known him. Not local, I mean."

"I've got some feelers out," Feargal said, taking the twig Moonbeam had brought him and tossing it back into the undergrowth for her to find. "Our Ferdinand seems a bit of a mystery man. He's been working for a firm of accountants in Dudley for the last six months, but can't find anything out about him before that."

"Do you think he changed his name?" Emerald's mouth fell open.

"That's pretty weird - a new identity ... Can he be in Witness Protection?"

"Or lived abroad?"

"I'll have to chivvy the troops to find out more. It's a bit of a poser alright."

"He was obviously quite adept at whizzing about the tracks, and had all the usual gear, so perhaps try some other mountain bike groups?" Tamsin suggested. As Feargal nodded, she grinned, "What about your mole in the police station, have you offended her?"

"Who said it's a *her*?" Feargal raised an eyebrow. "Actually my mole is on holiday, annoyingly."

"Your mole's gone to ground?" laughed Emerald.

And she and Tamsin both started making mole sounds, "Tssst! Tssst!" and laughing as they turned back to the road, knowing they'd all be meeting again the next day.

CHAPTER ELEVEN

Tamsin and Emerald arrived shortly before two the next day, and stood admiring the wreath hanging in the hedge that the Nighthawks had made for Ferdinand. It was an unusual wreath, made out of sticks, twigs, and ivy, in the shape of a wheel. There was a weak sun shining across it, so that it cast a strange long shadow across the hedge and the grass.

"That's like the things they make to line the route of the *Tour de France*," said Emerald quietly. "I saw it on the telly - they make all sorts of things to look like bikes."

"Touching," Tamsin nodded. "Imaginative too."

"Welcome, ladies," said a warm voice as they turned away from the wheel, finding themselves greeted by a tall man with greying hair. "I'm Jim Hansom, Nighthawks Club Secretary, and this is my wife Gillian."

As they all nodded and shook hands, Gillian said "Are you the two young ladies who found the .. er .. found Ferdinand? That must have been an awful shock!"

"Yes, we are. And it was! So when we heard you were having a memorial, we felt we simply had to show up and pay our respects."

"I guess you all knew him well, him being another cyclist?" asked Emerald.

"Actually, no, we didn't know him at all," Gillian began.

"Usually if people want to join us for a ride they come and announce themselves at the start," Jim took up the story. "But the first we knew of this awful thing was when the police came asking questions the next day. We were all right up the North Hill when it apparently happened."

"We hadn't realised there'd be so many spectators for the fireworks," added a stocky sandy-haired young man with a freckly nose as he joined them. "So once we'd struggled through the crowds we decided to avoid the Beacon for the night. I'm Adam, by the way, and this is Django," he grabbed his companion by the elbow, and Django, tall and lean where his friend was short and square, and dark in contrast with Adam's fair colouring - turned and matched Adam's friendly smile.

The group was growing now, and Jim and Gillian drifted off to do more clubby greetings.

Tamsin grabbed the chance to grill Adam and Django. "So you're Nighthawks, yeah?"

"We are indeed! And Django's one of our stars. He's likely to qualify for the Worlds if he keeps it up." Django smiled down at them, showing a fine combination of smugness and humility.

"The Worlds?" Emerald looked dumb and blonde. The blonde part was easy, as below her woolly hat her swathe of silvery-blonde hair draped itself over her shoulders and down her back. Looking dumb was more of a challenge, but she was quite good at it, having found how useful it could be.

"The World Championships," he explained. "It's what we all aspire to."

"That's impressive!" she gave Django a broad smile, and he stood just a little bit taller.

"Do they have women at the Worlds?" asked Tamsin, slightly abrasively.

"Oh yes, they do. We haven't had a Nighthawk there yet, but we're hoping to - see those girls over there?"

They all turned to see three young women deep in conversation, heads together.

"That's Sally and Cynthia. And Majella. They're all battling it out at the top of our group. I think Majella may make it through to qualifying before long. She's a tough nut! Single-minded. No time for anything but racing."

"You're a really serious group, then?" Emerald's eyelashes did a bit of batting.

As Adam nodded proudly, Tamsin added, "and how good was Ferdinand? Was *he* going places?"

"That's the funny thing. We've all turned up to honour the fellow, cos he died on our ride. But no-one seems to have known him. He was just another poacher," Adam said sadly.

"Poacher?" asked Emerald, looking puzzled.

"Yeah, not entitled to be on the ride," Django was happy to explain to Emerald, in his deep resonant voice. "Happens all the time, people just getting in on something without paying their dues."

"Is it possible he was killed by mistake? Those helmets you wear cover most of the face, don't they?" Emerald went on.

"Oh no, apparently he wasn't wearing a lid. Just an ordinary helmet. No chin guard or anything. So his face would be easy to see. That's what the police said when they interviewed me, anyway," he added hastily.

"Was he trying to infiltrate the group for some reason?" Tamsin raised an enquiring eyebrow. "He had all the gear on .."

"He wasn't wearing armour, it seems. Could have saved his life."

"Armour?" asked Emerald, beginning to feel like the legendary Greek nymph Echo, who could only repeat what others said. She wondered for a moment, if the Furies had another sister, called Echo.

"Body protection. Most people wear elbow protectors, some wear full chest armour."

Emerald shuddered. "From what we saw, that may not have saved him."

Tamsin put a hand on Emerald's arm, as Adam blustered, "Most awfully sorry - didn't want to remind you .. must have been ghastly."

"It's ok - really," said Tamsin. "So why was he here?"

"That's what we don't know. He was asking questions at *Flying*

Pedals apparently. Brenda was saying. But we just don't know why he was here - incognito, as it were."

"A real mystery man - don't you all mix, different groups, different places, you know?"

"Oh yes, we do - but no-one seems to know Ferdinand. I don't even know how they found out who he was - do you think the police found some id on him?"

"I'd never thought of that," lied Tamsin fluently. "I guess they must have done."

"By the way," Emerald dumbed and blonded again, having found how well it worked on Django, "is Ambrose here?" She peered around the group, as if to spot him.

"Ambrose?" Django looked nonplussed. "Oh, you must mean Andrew. There's an Andrew who comes up sometimes," he looked around the groups of figures, "don't think he's here though."

"Oh yes, Andrew! That's who I meant!"

"Now Django, you can't hog our visitors all to yourself!" Johnny Lightholder clapped an arm round Django's shoulder, steering him slightly away from Tamsin and Emerald and insinuating himself between. Emerald flinched and ducked to the other side of Tamsin and started to ask Adam some more questions about the World Championships.

"There's someone I'd like you to meet," said Adam, taking in the situation at a glance - a situation he was well used to, it seemed - pointing towards the group of young women cyclists he'd mentioned earlier. Emerald smiled gratefully at him, and looked round in time to see Django throwing Johnny's hand off him and staring close into his face and muttering something under his breath before turning on his heel with a flourish and marching away, leaving the other man standing alone.

"No love lost there?" said Tamsin quietly.

"Ah, Johnny's a bit full of himself," said Adam dismissively. "Don't mind him." And they joined Sally, Cynthia, and Majella. "I'd like you to meet er, Tamsin and .."

"Emerald!" Emerald helped him out.

"Emerald, sorry, yes! They were asking about women mountain bikers, and I thought they should hear it all from the horse's mouth, as it were," he laughed, gave a small bow, and left them to it.

"I saw you avoiding our Mr.Lightholder very skilfully!" smiled Cynthia.

"I already had to avoid him once already, in the shop. He fancies himself, right?"

"He's about the only person who does," said Sally, and the three women laughed knowingly.

Majella added, "He actually has a wife, though we never see her. She's probably sick of him too."

Tamsin opened her mouth to ask a polite question about women mountain biking when Cynthia said, "Who's that guy over there?"

They all turned to look as Feargal strode up the path into the gathering, and was greeted by Jim. By mutual consent, he and Tamsin 'didn't know each other'. This had worked well in the past and would probably help now.

"Not a Nighthawk?" asked Tamsin.

"Not seen him before."

"Perhaps he wants to join you - heard about this at the bike shop?" suggested Emerald.

"He can join me any day," laughed Majella, "he's hot!"

Tamsin sneezed and blew her nose to cover her giggles - that was one to tease Feargal with later! But could be very handy for him to get accepted by the bikers.

Jim coughed loudly and held up a hand. "Ladies and Gentlemen," he intoned, in the strange monotone adopted by vicars starting a service, "we're gathered here today to honour the memory of one who aspired to be one of us. Cyclists are a tight community, and though we didn't know Ferdinand Glossop, he had come to ride with us and so we feel it right to remember him. As you can see, Brenda and Gillian made a lovely wreath for him."

The groups of bikers murmured, then all stilled as they listened.

"I think a minute's silence would be appropriate here." He coughed again and bowed his head, hands folded in front of him, so that he could keep an eye on his watch ticking off the seconds.

They all stood quietly, most looking down, but Tamsin and Feargal taking the opportunity to study all of them by turn.

Another cough and everyone relaxed and started moving again. "Thank you all for coming. Gillian has the register for the next meet, if you'd like to put your names down?"

The mood lightened as everyone felt they had done their bit in respecting the memory of this unknown person and they could now put it behind them. The three girls gave Tamsin and Emerald a nod and a smile as they headed over to sign up with Gillian, so they walked back towards Adam, now talking animatedly to Feargal.

"*Flying Pedals* is the place to go to upgrade your bike. There's not much they don't know about bikes!" he enthused. "There's Mark," he added, pointing out the mechanic as he walked past them. "He's one of their grease monkeys."

"Ah, yes," Feargal said, "I've seen him there," and he turned back quickly to Adam. "So tell me about your next ride."

Tamsin tuned out as she looked at a small huddle of men near the wheel wreath. They were deep in conversation, looking quite conspiratorial. She recognised Johnny and Django, but didn't know the other two. As they stood, heads together, Tamsin saw one of the strangers pass a small parcel to Johnny, who slipped it quickly into his pocket.

"Did you see that?" she whispered to Emerald.

"Very fishy!" she whispered back. "Wonder who they are? Could one of them be Ambrose?"

As Tamsin and Emerald approached the group, they began to pick up scraps of the conversation: "... you sure it was him?" Johnny was asking.

"Positive," replied Django firmly and quietly. "I'd recognise those beady eyes anywhere."

"Who are they talking about?" Emerald whispered to Tamsin.

"No idea. Let's find out," Tamsin replied, her detective nose beginning to twitch. She moved closer to the group, and sidled up behind Django.

"Hey," Johnny said, noticing Tamsin and Emerald hovering. "This is private."

Tamsin was about to speak up, but Django put in. "It's okay, Johnny, they're cool. They're with Adam." Tamsin let this misunderstanding run and slotted in beside Django.

Johnny looked at Tamsin and Emerald suspiciously, then shrugged. "Fine. But if anything gets out, we'll know where it came from."

Tamsin exchanged a worried look with Emerald as they moved closer to each other. The two men that they didn't recognise stared at them, and Tamsin did not like the look of them at all.

"So what's going on?" Tamsin asked, trying to sound casual.

Django stepped forward. "We think there's someone spying on us."

"Spying?" Emerald repeated, looking around nervously.

Johnny nodded. "Yeah. We've been getting some strange vibes lately. Like someone's watching us."

Tamsin looked puzzled, but before she could open her mouth, "Racing," said one of the unfamiliar men, a tall bloke with a bushy beard. Tamsin wondered how he fitted it in under his helmet chin-guard. "We've got a race coming up next month, and we think someone's trying to sabotage us."

"Sabotage?" Emerald said, her eyes widening, Echo-ing again.

"Yeah," said Johnny. "We've had some close calls at competitions lately. Like someone's been messing about with the route before our runs. There've been some nasty falls."

Tamsin looked around at the group as a light came on in her mind. She felt that this may explain what had happened to Ferdinand. Perhaps he was a spy! Or he was mistaken for one. "So what are you going to do?" she asked.

"We're going to catch them," declared Django. "We've got a plan." The men all drew back and clammed up. Clearly they weren't going to divulge their plan to strangers, so Tamsin nodded and turned away from the group. "We'll leave you to it, then," she smiled.

"What was all that about?" Emerald asked when they'd got a few paces away, her eyes wide.

Tamsin shook her head, trying to work out the connection between what she'd just heard, and why they were all there this afternoon. "I have no idea," she said finally. "But I think we might be on to something. There has to be a link between this and the murder."

Emerald nodded, "Too much of a coincidence," she said. "Here, let's find Feargal and get out of here. I'm suddenly not feeling very welcome, quite honestly."

Feargal saw them and began winding up his conversation with the ever-friendly Adam, and as they started down the path they waved their goodbyes to Jim and Gillian.

Feargal caught up with them on the path after a couple of hundred yards. As they were far out of earshot of the group, Feargal said, "Well? What did you learn?"

"Loads! And you?"

"Plenty," he nodded.

"Let's debrief over a coffee at Pippin Lane. I'm feeling the need of some canine comfort."

"And a warm-up!" added Emerald, pulling her hat down over her ears. "This winter sun doesn't do much to counteract the cold ground. But I'm glad to be away from that creepy Johnny Lightholder."

"Definitely. It's all been pretty weird."

"Weird." Never had Emerald Echo-ed a truer word.

CHAPTER TWELVE

"Well, you certainly made a stir!" Tamsin passed a mug of steaming hot chocolate to Feargal. They were all relaxing in the living room with the fire on full blast in an attempt to warm them up after standing about at Ferdinand's memorial for so long.

Feargal raised an enquiring eyebrow as he gratefully accepted the mug.

"Majella thinks you're *hot!*" laughed Tamsin, as she wiggled into her armchair beside Moonbeam. "Budge up, Moonbeam!"

"She's pretty hot herself," Feargal said dreamily, then, noticing Emerald's expression, said, "Just kidding. Not my type."

"Fit though," said Emerald appreciatively. "Strong enough ..."

"Can't dismiss the female of the species as our murderer?" asked Feargal. "You're right. They're tough cookies, those mountain bikers. Not squeamish, I'd say."

"Are you going to join the Nighthawks for a ride?" Emerald asked, as ever stroking Opal who'd taken ownership of her lap as soon as she had sat down.

"I am. That Adam fellow told me where to present myself on

Wednesday evening. I reckon I'll be able to pick up some info. What the connection is, you know."

"Do you have a bike? And all the gear?"

"What a question! Yes, I have a bike, and whatever I don't own I'll acquire before Wednesday night. Need to look the part!" Feargal smiled smugly.

Tamsin related to him what the men had been saying about sabotage and spies.

"*And*," said Emerald with emphasis, "one of the ones we didn't know passed Johnny a parcel which he pocketed fast."

"Now that is definitely suspicious!"

"It could have been innocuous, of course. A new pair of bicycle clips or whatever it is they use," Tamsin grinned. "But there was something furtive about the exchange."

"Fishy. There was no sign of an Ambrose," said Emerald.

"Or any knowledge of him, apparently."

"Let's look at what we've got," said Feargal, getting out his notebook and tapping his pen against his teeth. "Possibilities: Ferdinand was a spy wanting to sabotage the Nighthawks. Ferdinand was looking for Ambrose because .. er .. say, Ambrose had run off with his girlfriend. Or, Ferdinand was an investigator of some kind, and was looking into cheating."

"Or drugs. Or fraud," interjected Tamsin.

"Or drugs. Or fraud, perhaps unconnected with cycling, but cycling was the only way he could reach … whoever it was he was trying to track down."

"It doesn't help a lot," Emerald looked glum, and kissed the top of Opal's purring head.

"Think. Why would *you* want to infiltrate an organisation secretly?"

"Um," Emerald thought hard, "in my case it would be a personal thing. Wanting to put something right. But in Tamsin's case, I could imagine her getting caught up in investigating some evil deed. Like fraud, or cheating. She's more altruistic than me!"

"Maybe he was trying to track someone down from his past, and he was following up the last lead he had. But the stakes were obviously very high. It does suggest something more than personal interest," mused Feargal. "Oh hallo Quiz, have you come to say hallo?"

"What do you think of this package-passing? Red herring?" Emerald twirled her hair round her index finger.

"I had thought performance drugs of some kind," Feargal unconsciously twirled Quiz's ear as he watched Emerald. "And exposing that would certainly sabotage the chances for any of them to get into the higher levels of competition. I don't know about mountain biking in particular, but most sports are very hot on this."

Banjo provided some light relief by losing his ball on a rope he'd been happily bouncing, and scrabbling under the bookcase again to reach it, so Tamsin sent Moonbeam to help him out.

"Sometimes people can't manage something on their own," Feargal murmured, watching the joint effort at recovering the ball. "Hey, supposing Ferdinand had a sidekick?" Finding himself warming up fast, he pulled up the sleeves of his thick jumper.

"There's been no sign of one so far," Tamsin plucked some under-the-bookcase fluff off the ball before tossing it back to Banjo to bounce and catch again.

"Ferdinand was a youngish bloke," said Emerald. "I bet he had a girl in tow."

"It would be great if we could find her! How on earth can we find that out?" Tamsin looked enquiringly at Feargal.

"Ok, ok. I'll check with my contacts on the paper, see what we can find. Someone presumably will want to bury him?"

"You find out about his family, where he's from, and all the rest. Nuisance, your mole being AWOL. We'll talk to Sara a bit more, now we have a little more information. I'd like to ask that Johnny some questions. But we'd need to do it in a public place. I don't trust him an inch!"

Emerald jumped up in her seat, almost dislodging Opal, who looked grumpier than ever. "And you know who could help?"

"Charity!" Tamsin chuckled. "She's due back from Torquay any minute, and she'll be miffed she missed the drama. You're right, Em, Charity knows everyone. She's bound to have some background info on the bike shop and its denizens." And so saying, Tamsin buzzed Charity a text straight away, to find out when she'd be available for a pow-wow.

CHAPTER THIRTEEN

"Mind out Sapphire!" cried Tamsin as she waved her mug in the air to permit a second cat to clamber onto her lap, Charity having the third cat on hers, along with Muffin lying on the armchair seat beside her tiny owner. Tamsin always felt like a giant at Charity's.

In the cluttered but warm and cosy front parlour of Charity's little cottage, a small fire burned in the grate and all the cats and Muffin had clearly been sleeping on the plush rug in front of the hearth - till Tamsin's knock at the door had caused Muffin to jump up and run around holding her teddy bear, which she proudly presented to their visitor as she came in. The cats stayed where they were till Tamsin had sat down and then they decided they'd prefer her warm lap.

In the kitchen while Charity made the tea, Tamsin had heard all about the trip to Torquay, Charity's niece Sophie, the new baby, the raging sea in the Christmas storms and all the rest. So once they were sitting down Charity jumped in with, "So tell me, my dear, what *have* you been up to now?"

"I'm afraid I found another body, Charity. I didn't mean to! But he was there, right under our noses. Couldn't help it." She deliberated over the plate of homemade biscuits being offered, had a small but unequal battle in her head between her waistline and her greed, and guess what? Greed won and she bit into the crunchy but moist confection with pleasure. "You're only just back, Charity, and you've already been baking!"

"Nothing like being back in my own kitchen," Charity smiled. "And having found yourself a victim, Tamsin the Malvern Hills Detective wants to investigate, eh?" Charity smiled as Tamsin blushed. "And you want to pick my brains about these cyclists?"

"Charity, I have learnt that you know *everyone* and you know all about their family history too. You're the first person I thought of. There's a bunch of these people, whizzing about the Hills at night, and I don't know them at all."

"Righty-ho. Where will you start?"

"First of all, let me fill you in on what I know of the story so far." And Tamsin outlined the events to Charity - the fireworks, the finding of the fallen cyclist, Search and Rescue, the trip to *Flying Pedals,* Sara, Mark, and the memorial on the Hills. "So now, the *dramatis personae* .. Does the name Ferdinand Glossop mean anything to you?"

"The poor young man who died? Well, I was thinking about that when I read about him in the *Malvern Mercury.* There was an old family called Glossop out beyond Hereford - or was it Shropshire? - in the Welsh Marches. One of those families destroyed by the last war - they lost two sons, tragically. So Ferdinand could be a great-nephew or something."

"Or perhaps it was an assumed name and he's no relation."

"Goodness, that smells of skulduggery. Keep still, Muffy-muff dear. Your paws are digging into me."

"It seems there is skulduggery to root out," said Tamsin quietly and took another bite of the sensational biscuit. "I'll get Feargal to check out the Glossops."

"And next?"

"The next name I offer for your consideration is .. Jim Hansom, and his wife Gillian."

"Ah now, them I know. Jim's one of those people who likes to feel important. With that paunch I doubt if he does much riding, but he enjoys being the secretary of a society. He's got a small firm which funds his pleasant lifestyle - um .. accountancy, that's it. It's in Stourport, but they choose to live here in Malvern where Gillian's family is from. Here you are Mufflet, a morsel of biscuit for sitting so quietly. Who's a good girl then? He goes to those business breakfasts I hear."

"Really? However do you know that, Charity?"

"Dorothy! You remember Dorothy where you had a room when you first arrived in Malvern?" Tamsin nodded eagerly, thinking back a few years to when she first settled in Great Malvern, and murmured, "Of course". "Well she's running her house as a b&b now - so she goes to the business meetings sometimes, to keep in touch with developments in the town. Tourism and that sort of thing. Comes back with lots of gossip! Who are the movers and shakers, who's full of hot air, you know the sort of thing."

"A b&b? How enterprising of her!"

"Yes, it was something you said when you were lodging with her. Gave her the idea. You *can* teach an old dog new tricks, you know!" Charity smiled benignly.

Tamsin blushed and took a swig of her tea and a chomp of her biscuit. "I should be more careful about what I say," she laughed. "But I'm delighted for her - she got plenty of experience keeping me under control when I stayed with her! And it was she who said I could get Quiz while I was there, remember? Definitely a good egg. So .. Jim is someone who likes to be busy and feel needed."

"Exactly. And Gillian's the same. She's involved in the Nighthawks, and she's also active in the Women's Institute, the Townswomen's Guild, the Malvern Shelter, and other such worthy organisations."

"So - upright citizens, probably blameless?"

"I would think so. Though there would be plenty of scope for fiddling the books in all these places, as he knows all about numbers ..."

"Ok. I'll keep him in. Now, the bike shop. *Flying Pedals*. Seems to be a social hub for cyclists in the area. Local bike shop with aspirations. What do you know of Howard and Brenda, and their son Jason?"

"Fairly standard small-town family business, I would say. Howard bought the shop when it was a ramshackle place run by an old fellow who mended pushbikes. He developed it into a specialist shop for serious cyclists as well as catering for the existing clientele with sit-up-and-beg bikes with wicker baskets on the handlebars."

"That would be more my style!" Tamsin detached Sapphire's claws from her trouser-leg and adjusted her position so that the purring cat could knead the cushion instead of her thigh.

"Brenda, as you probably know, is very jolly and the perfect front-of-house person. Howard really does *not* have the common touch! As for Jason, I don't know too much about him. Hasn't been in much trouble so far as I know. He's been done for drunk and disorderly I do know, and I think he feels trapped in the family business. Bit resentful. Has a need to cut loose, hence the drinking thing."

"He does seem a bit sour, I must say, though I only saw him for a moment or two."

"Wouldn't you be a bit sour with Howard as a father?"

"Point taken. But the business seems to be doing well. Do you know how much some of those performance bikes cost? I saw a couple at eight grand!"

"Eight thousand pounds? Good Heavens. I had no idea it was such an expensive hobby."

"I don't think it's a hobby for many of the Nighthawks - it's deadly serious. It's a vocation - a mission to reach the top. Be top daredevil! So now .. the riders - I don't have full names, but here are some that I met - Adam, Django, Majella, Cynthia, and .. er .. Sally. Those are all the names I got."

"Adam .. Would he be a stocky sandy-haired man?"

"Yes, that's him. Know him?"

"His father was the vicar at a few of the local parishes. You know how they bunch them together these days and they become a kind of roving parson? And if I've got it right, the boy was always good at sports - won all the school medals at Worcester Grammar."

"He certainly was very polite - nicely spoken. Seemed a good type to me."

"I'd be surprised if he was anything else, to be honest. What was the next name?"

"Django."

"Djan-go?" Charity tried out the unusual name as if she were tasting a rare wine. "No, never heard of him. Strange name. Is he keen on the guitar?" Charity looked at Tamsin's baffled face and said, "Ah, before your time, dear. Jazz."

Tamsin had a sudden vision of Charity at a jazz club back in her heyday, wearing a red cocktail dress, tortoiseshell cigarette holder in hand, and mixing with exotic musicians. She shook her head and banished the thought, saying, "Majella, Cynthia, Sally?"

"Majella. Now that's an Irish name. I wonder if she would be one of the O'Donovan girls. There are three of them. Grainne plays tennis for Worcestershire, Concepta is a swimmer. Super-athletic family. I don't know how the parents managed to take them to all their different practises and lessons when they were younger. Must have been a full-time job for them. Very dedicated. Their father was a professional snooker player. Good hand-eye co-ordination runs in the family, I imagine."

"How interesting. Was their mother a sportswoman too? I imagine she must have spent half her life tending the washing machine, with all those sporty kits to launder!"

"I remember her at the tennis club - ooh, back in the day," Charity sighed as she remembered her own sportier days.

Tamsin moved them on. "Majella is the great hope to reach high honours in the women's side of the sport, apparently. It seems that this mountain biking is very tough. They have to be strong. That's why I'm not counting out the women. Know the other two? Cynthia and Sally?"

Charity shook her head.

"Oh, and there's another man. Johnny Lightholder."

"Hah! Johnny Lightholder, eh?" said Charity, tossing her head back and laughing. "Now there's lots I can tell you about Johnny Lightholder!"

Tamsin took another chomp of biscuit and settled back to hear the story.

"The Lightholders lived in Trotley. Not here in Nether Trotley, but in Middle Trotley, which is rather larger - lots of council houses there. The Lightholders were one of those families that were always checked out first whenever there was a small crime in the area. On first-name terms with the police, they were. They'd pinch anything that wasn't nailed down. There were three boys and several girls too. Their father Freddie was known locally as Freddie Lightfingers. But they were a necessary evil I suppose. You know there are animals that are parasitic but very useful?"

"Like Cleaner Fish, and Egrets? Just how much do we owe to David Attenborough!" Tamsin laughed.

"Remarkable man," agreed Charity. "Yes, just like that. If you ever had an old dead car you wanted rid of, you'd call the Lightholders. They were happy to take it for scrap. I had an old caravan once that I wanted gone. The whole family - of raggle-taggle small boys, larger cousins, and girls in faded frocks that were too large or too small for them - turned out to push it away. But I got a promise out of Freddie before I let him take it. That I'd expect consideration in return."

"And did he keep his promise?"

"He did. There is honesty among thieves, it seems, and I never had anything stolen or "borrowed" ever after that."

"So Johnny Lightholder was brought up wide of the law, but has some morals built in?"

"Perhaps. I hear he's quite a womaniser."

"So it seems. He made an unwelcome pass at Emerald and gave her the creeps. The women bikers made reference to his wandering hands too."

"Well, if there's trouble or shady dealings about, I'd expect young Johnny to be right in the thick of it."

"What's your instinct telling you about this, Charity? Why do you think Ferdinand was murdered?"

Charity shifted her tabby cat's position and slipped another piece of biscuit to Muffin. "It seems to me that he was poking his nose in where it wasn't wanted. And from what you told me, I'd guess that involved the usual things - sex, money, or reputation."

Tamsin counted on her fingers, "One, someone stole Ferdinand's girl. Two, someone stole Ferdinand's money. And three, Ferdinand was a threat to someone - had some knowledge they didn't want put about. That leaves us with jealousy and revenge - two powerful emotions, theft or blackmail - again, strong motives, or a cover-up. Fits in with possible drugs or tampering. I'd love to find something that narrowed it down a bit! Once we have a motive, wouldn't that make it easier to unearth the rest and track down the killer?"

And as she polished off a third biscuit, Tamsin had no idea how quickly she was to get a huge leap forward in the case.

CHAPTER FOURTEEN

Tamsin was doing one of her favourite things - drinking coffee in The Cake Stop, with Quiz at her side, a friend sitting opposite her, and a huge slice of one of The Furies' best cakes waiting for her to tuck in to.

The friend was Sara. They were meeting before Emerald's Tuesday evening class in the upper room, and soon a flood of yoga students would arrive with their yoga bags, mats, and towels. They wouldn't eat cake before class (though Tamsin had it on good authority that they came and wolfed it down at other times) so she wanted to despatch her treat before they got there.

Sara had been putting in some extra hours at *Flying Pedals* while she was on her Christmas break, and wanted to report her latest discoveries to Tamsin. Slim as she was, she was not eating cake before her class. But she had plenty to tell Tamsin while she munched hers.

"I was checking up on this Ambrose guy, in the sales history, you know. Remember Feargal suggested looking up Irish names? Well I found an A. O'Brien from two years back. Buying a new mountain bike and all the trimmings. It could be him, yes?" Sara spoke eagerly.

"It could," said Tamsin as she finished her mouthful of cake, and offered a morsel to Quiz who had been waiting patiently.

"And," Sara wriggled forward in her chair, "know what else I found?"

"Go on!"

"F. Glossop. Also two years ago, on the same day and *almost the same time*. He was getting a new pump and a spare tube. The sale was rung up two minutes after Ambrose's." She sat back again triumphantly.

"So ... ?"

"So that suggests they were in the shop together! They must have known each other then."

"Of course! You're right - well done, Sara! Ferdinand was perhaps introducing Ambrose to mountain biking. And the friends fell out?"

"I wonder ..." Sara lost focus as she craned her neck to see the people coming through the large front door of The Cake Stop.

"And I wonder .. This Ambrose fella - he has an Irish name and likes cycling. Wonder if there's a link with the other Irish family - Majella's."

"I've seen Majella in the shop a couple of times. Never with a bloke." Sara finished off her coffee as she glanced towards the front door again. "Talking of blokes, Mark seems to have taken a shine to me."

"He's nice enough, but with, shall we say, a chequered past."

"Oh, I'm not interested in him. And I can see he's working hard to turn his life around, hopefully. But I thought it would be easy to get information from him if we needed it."

"That's true, and anyway, you're spoken for, aren't you?" Tamsin raised an enquiring eyebrow.

Sara blushed, and looked towards the door again as more people arrived. "Ah, here he is now!" Her tense shoulders dropped and her face became a relaxed, smiley, happy one as she saw Andrew coming in, his yoga bag over his shoulder. He looked around the café, spotted Sara and loped over to their table. He's like a big puppy, thought Tamsin to herself, as he greeted them warmly and pulled up a chair. Fortunately several other yoga students arrived and swarmed over to join them, so that Tamsin could leave Sara and Andrew in peace.

"Hello Tamsin - oh Quiz!" Cameron jumped up and down with excitement as Molly tried to park him at the table and went to the counter to order drinks for them.

Tamsin was always pleased to meet Chas's delightful young family, and shuffled her chair along so that they could fit in two more chairs, for himself and his mother. Cameron plonked himself right next to Quiz so he could ruffle her ears as she liked, her big head on his lap.

"Have you heard about the latest *murder?*" his childish voice continued in a stage whisper.

"I have!" Tamsin smiled at his boyish enthusiasm.

"I'm a cyclist, you know?" he said proudly. "Daddy and Mummy gave me classes for my birthday."

"And what birthday would that be?" asked Shirley as she pulled up a chair next to Cameron.

"My tenth!" he said, drawing himself up to his full four foot six.

"And what are these classes?"

"Cycling profij, er Cycling profesh, er .."

"Bike training!" Tamsin helped him out. "Excellent."

"You see," Cameron said earnestly, leaning towards Tamsin, "some wizard riders come to help teach us. It's awfully good! Oh, thank you Mum!" He turned his attention to the slice of cake that had appeared in front of him as his mother sat down beside him with his hot chocolate and her black coffee.

"Some of the Nighthawks volunteer to help the kids on Sunday afternoons," Molly explained. "Looking for recruits, I'll bet!"

Cameron chewed his first mouthful of cake, the icing festooning his upper lip. He waved his fork around to keep their attention till he could speak. "There's a few who come quite a lot. They're really cool!"

"What are their names?"

"Um .." He had to work his way through another mouthful. "Cynthia, and Adam sometimes. They're really nice. But Django's the best! He's just so cool! And he'll be in the World Championships soon. That's what I want to do," he added with a dreamy look in his eye. "He's a bit soppy about Majella though," the little boy shuddered meaningfully and stabbed another forkful of cake.

"He is?" prompted Tamsin.

"Yeah. He looks at her all funny. Bit like Mum and Dad when they think we're not there."

Molly snorted into her coffee. "What a pet you are," she smiled at her young son.

So Django and Majella are a thing, thought Tamsin. Or perhaps Django wishes they were a thing? "Is Majella soppy about Django back?" she asked the little boy.

"Nah," said Cameron dismissively, now concentrating on his cake and chocolate. "Have I got time to finish this before class," he asked his mother anxiously. And at her nod he said "Oh goodo," and tucked in greedily.

The space round the table filled up with more of Emerald's students, gratefully removing their thick coats and hats as they felt the warmth of the busy cafe. Sara tore her attention away from Andrew to greet her friend Julia who would be giving her and her bike a lift back to Bishop's Green after class.

Then, "Hey Tamsin," Sara said excitedly. "Andrew's got a race on Saturday, over in the Forest of Dean. It's a qualifier - everyone will be there. I thought," she added in a quieter voice, "since I've done extra days this week - I thought I'd ask Brenda for Saturday off so I can go."

"The Forest of Dean?" said Tamsin. "Nice walking there ... hmm, wonder if my dogs would enjoy a visit to the Forest on Saturday. Whaddya think, Quiz?" Quiz's tail thumped as her ears both stood up with interest.

"Here's a flyer," Andrew fished a slightly battered and crumpled sheet from his pocket and handed it to Tamsin. "There's parking laid on. You can't miss it - it'll be packed!"

Tamsin pocketed the flyer with a smile, and with Cameron engrossed in his cake, she turned to Shirley who, as well as being Mark's much-harassed mother who had bailed him out of so many scrapes, had also been a student with her Pyrenean Mountain Dog at Tamsin's ill-fated Nether Trotley classes.

"Shirley - how's Luke doing? He must be getting huge by now."

Shirley's face lighted up. "Oh yes, he is big, but still so gentle." She nodded towards Quiz, now dozing on her mat between Tamsin and Cameron. "He's a lot bigger than her now! I must say I feel very safe with him in the house."

"I bet! But Mark's living at home now, isn't he? I hear he's doing very well at *Flying Pedals*."

"Yes, thank you Tamsin. He's loving it there. Never happier than when he's messing about with wheels and oily rags," she hooted her shy laugh.

"And what does he have to say about our bike murder?"

Shirley drew herself back as if stung, and snapped, "Oh Mark had nothing to do with that!"

"No no, of course not. Not at all. I just thought - he may pick things up, you know, being with all those bike enthusiasts all the time."

"He's not said anything to me. You know," she leaned closer to Tamsin, "he really likes Brenda, but he's not mad about that Howard." She pursed her lips, nodded sagely, and sat back in her chair again, the subject apparently closed.

Emerald came down the stairs from the upper room and gathered her excited flock. They were much more relaxed without the lurking presence of Kurt, who had usually stood guard at the bottom of those stairs. Julia said quietly, "No Kurt." They all paused for a moment and looked at their drinks.

"Bet he misses his cat, said Cameron sadly. They don't allow them in loony bins, do they?"

"Secure hospitals, I believe they call them," Molly corrected him. "And no, I think not."

And as Tamsin gathered her hat, coat, and dog, and waved them all goodbye, she wondered if they would be helping another person into a secure hospital, on their way to finding out who had murdered Ferdinand Glossop.

CHAPTER FIFTEEN

"What's the news? How did you get on last night?" Tamsin had rung Feargal on Thursday morning, eager to hear all the latest.

"Lot to tell you actually - can we meet?"

Tamsin flipped through her diary pages. "I've got an eleven in Upton-upon-Severn, back here for a walk then a three on the Pershore road. Someone who insists her young puppy should only have two meals a day and wonders why he keeps crying and chewing things up ... mad. How about Jean-Philippe's at two? I'll have all the dogs with me."

"I'd love to see all the dogs! Two at The Cake Stop then." And he rang off, in a hurry as always.

Her eleven o'clock went very well. It was someone who simply needed to stop saying NO to her dog whenever she saw him, and who was amazed at the results Tamsin got so fast with a different attitude. So she arrived at the café with Quiz, Banjo, and Moonbeam, in high spirits. As she went to the counter, Kylie smiled and nodded to the back of the shop where Feargal had commandeered a table with lots of space behind for all the dog mats, and on the table were two steaming mugs.

"Nearly forgot!" Kylie called after her. "There's a children's party in the Upper room this afternoon, so if Emerald arrives early for her new class I might still be clearing up."

"I'll tell her, Kylie - thanks!"

And thanks were due again as she arrived at the table with her coffee waiting for her. "Oh thank you!" said Tamsin as the dogs greeted their friend then settled on their mats. The snow and ice had long gone and had been replaced with rain and mud, so she was careful to keep the dogs' paws off laps and on their beds. She pulled an old towel out of her dog bag and gave twelve paws and two swishing tails a quick rub. At last, she peeled off her waterproof and sat opposite Feargal with a sigh, wrapping her damp, slightly red, hands round her coffee mug to warm them up.

"What have you been up to today, Feargal?"

"Recovering from last night's exertions! I'm pretty stiff, I can tell you. So I've been knocking around the office. Doing some research."

"Into?"

"Into Jim Hansom's business venture."

"Oh, really? That's interesting! What prompted this particular investigation?"

Feargal removed his hand from Quiz's wet head and leant forward, elbows on the table. "I heard Adam having a go at Jim last night. He was asking what the delay was on the Nighthawks accounts. Jim looked really uncomfortable. I couldn't hear what the delay was, but he was very defensive about it."

"What did Adam say?"

"I couldn't earwig too obviously. But he said something about Jim needing to get a move on and stomped off. I got the impression this was not the first time of asking."

"So you're checking out his official business for funny figures?"

"I am. And I'm waiting for a couple of reports to come back from colleagues who cover Stourport."

"Stourport-on-Severn? Ah yes, Charity said he has his accountancy business there."

"Yes. So being an accountant, it's a bit fishy that he's prevaricating over the bike club's accounts." He looked into Moonbeam's appealing brown eyes. "I'm sure your tiny paws are dry by now, Moonbeam. Probably too tiny to have got wet in the first place. You are like a little fairy the way you trit-trot along. Hop up!" and the little dog in her fleecy jumper floated up lightly onto his lap and settled there to warm up.

"So what else did you learn last night, O intrepid reporter?"

"There was a lot of excitement about these qualifiers on Saturday. It's in the Forest of Dean, on the hills over towards Wales."

"I know! I'll be there with this lot," she nodded towards the now-slumbering damp dogs. "Andrew's having a go, and Sara will be cheering him on."

"Django is also 'having a go' as you put it - only he's deadly serious about it. And so is Majella. Now there's naked ambition ..."

"I got the impression she'd let nothing stand in the way of her success. Just a way with her."

"They're both dead keen. And it seems Django is a bit keen on Majella too. But she's not having any of it."

"She thinks you're hot, remember?"

"She *was* a bit flirty, it's true. But I think that may have been for Django's benefit." He shifted Moonbeam's sharp elbows slightly on his lap. "Anyhow, while I was thrashing about the Hills I had to stop and adjust my chain. Cynthia stopped to see if I needed help. Seems they're very supportive of each other in the Nighthawks. Will always stop to help a downed biker."

"She seems to be in cahoots with Adam, I believe .."

"Apparently so. Well as we were fixing my bike I chatted to her, of course. And as we got it working again, I said I'd heard the name Ambrose and asked where he was. What a response I got! She clammed up instantly, and said, 'You'll have to ask Majella about that,' snapped her visor down, stood up on her pedals and cycled away fast."

"So the mention of Ambrose hits a nerve. Interesting! Wish we knew who he was."

"They drop into the Pig and Bucket after the meet usually. Catch a quick round before closing time. I'll make a point of going there next week and seeing what I can learn."

"You'll go again?"

"Yeah, I will. Actually, I really enjoyed it! In fact, I'd go so far as to say it was quite exhilarating. Though I think I'll be struggling to walk tomorrow!" He stretched out his legs ruefully, catching hold of Moonbeam so she didn't slither off.

"Ok. So we have Jim being shifty about the club's money. Majella teasing Django. Cynthia very upset at the mention of Ambrose. Wonder if there was something going on there?"

"Hmm. And everyone at fever pitch about Saturday. I'm glad you're going. I have a footie match I have to cover or I'd come too. It's the Worcester Wolves - important match for them against the Solihull Sliders."

"Sounds epic," Tamsin smirked. "So we'll both be stamping our feet in the cold! I'll lurk and chatter and be curious. See if I can get anyone to open up. Ooh, look at the time! I have to get back to dry these dogs off at home and pick up the van and go."

"Another dog to be saved!" Feargal laughed.

"And another dog family to have their lives transformed," Tamsin smiled in return, as she assembled her troops, rolled up their mats and stuffed them in her bag, and headed out into the cold drizzle again.

CHAPTER SIXTEEN

Saturday was just as cold as the preceding couple of weeks, but there was a strong wind which had blown away the relentless drizzle of the last few days.

"You'll need to wrap up warm," Tamsin filled her flask with steaming hot soup and packed it into her backpack with mugs and some brown bread rolls.

"That smells good," said Emerald, winding a long scarf round and round her swan-like neck.

"You'll be glad of it after a couple of hours freezing on a Gloucestershire hillside!"

"I will. Won't the dogs get cold, standing about?" Emerald parked Opal on the worktop while she bent to address Quiz and Banjo.

"They'll be fine. That's the sort of terrain they were bred for - and of course I'll run them first to warm them up, away from the track."

"Ooh, what's this?" Emerald scooped up a tiny pink knitted jumper and held it up to admire.

"New jumper for Moonbeam! She does feel the cold, having no woolly undercoat. Charity made it for me. I think she was using up the wool she was using for her niece's baby. Isn't it cute?"

"Oh, it is! Look at the embroidery - I love the little moon with its beams. You'll be the Belle of the Bicycle Track, Moonbeam." Emerald eased the jumper over the little dog's head and threaded her front legs into the sleeves. "There - a perfect fit! Clever Charity. I wonder what we'll find out today," she said as she stood up to admire her handiwork and Moonbeam posed, wondering what to make of this strange new garment.

"I'm hoping to get a bit of a feel for what's going on there. And I'm itching to find out why Ambrose is such a touchy subject."

"Perhaps Andrew will learn something too." And they set to loading the van with their picnic lunch, the dogs, and all their leads and harnesses.

"Aren't we meant to take blankets in the car in winter?" Emerald frowned, peering behind the seats.

"This van is bursting with blankets! Though they may smell somewhat of dog. We'll be fine."

Tamsin parked on the other side of the hill that the track was on, and they got out and started the ascent of the hill so that the dogs could have a good run around in the Forest.

"Is that a deer?" Emerald pointed her gloved fingers at a dark shape leaping through the undergrowth.

Tamsin just had time to scoop Moonbeam up in her arms while she called "Down!" to the bigger dogs. Once she was sure they wouldn't chase she released them all. "Yep. Muntjac. Funny little things. They live on their own, like cats. And they have tusks." They scrambled up a steep incline and she puffed, "This is warming me up too!"

And when they emerged through the trees at the summit they saw the track laid out below them, covering the side of the hill, weaving through trees, round bushes, and over gaps and other such hazards. The coloured tapes and flags danced in the stiff wind. There seemed to be hundreds of people there already lower down the hill, the crowds wrapped up warm in jackets and hats, and the riders - many in colourful clothing - fiddling with their bikes, making last minute adjustments.

Tamsin could barely recognise the Nighthawks in their full kit, with lids, body armour, their bikes with the characteristic chunky tyres, stripped of anything unnecessary like mudguards - and bearing their number on the handlebars. With the feeling of excitement and anticipation in the air, it all suddenly became very real - and captivating!

"Look!" said Emerald, pointing down the track, "There's Sara!"

"Is that Andrew with her? I can't recognise him without his usual jeans and baggy jumper."

"I, on the other hand, am well aware of what he looks like in skin-tight lycra ..."

Tamsin stared at her for a moment. "Oh, yoga class!" she laughed as she cottoned on. "Look, they're coming up here."

They moved a little way down the hill to join their friends.

"Glad you managed to get the day off, Sara," Tamsin called out.

"So am I! It was a close one alright. Howard was really grumpy about letting me go, but Brenda interceded for me. I've been there all week. What does he want - blood?" Sara snorted.

"Strange - if that's the way he chooses to treat his employees," said Andrew, tipping up his helmet visor.

"There's a lot of strange people in this sport, if you ask me," Emerald chipped in, plunging her gloved hands deep into her pockets to keep them warm.

"Where are the rest of the Nighthawks?"

"They're in the collecting area, Tamsin, over that side." Andrew pointed across and down the hill, where the brightly-coloured tapes and flags fluttered and flapped in the cold wind which swept mercilessly up the hill. Lots of cyclists and their supporters were busying themselves preparing for their race, having their numbers checked by stewards with clipboards.

"Do they go up and then down, or do they start at the top?" This from Emerald, never shy of appearing dumb, which as everyone who knew her was well aware she emphatically was not!

"That's a great question, Emerald!" said Andrew, pleased to be able to explain. "They do both. First we have the cross-country event which goes up, down, and all over the place. It's a mass race event, lots of laps.

That's what I'm in. Then there's the downhill timed individual event. That's the qualifier, and what all the excitement is about."

"I can't wait!" said Sara excitedly. "I've never been to a bike race before."

"This terrain looks really difficult - you wouldn't find me trying to cycle on it!" Tamsin said with feeling. "Look at all those tree roots there - that would give you a bumpy ride alright. And that drop over there!"

"And wouldn't you skid on all that gravel?"

"And the fallen leaves too? Do people get hurt?"

"They can do," said Andrew, stroking his chin like an elderly professor, "but we're used to the bumps and bruises," he shrugged nonchalantly.

"Rather you than me! When do they start? You're in the first race, right?"

"Ye-e-e-s, I'd better be getting down there," he fiddled with his brake levers nervously. "Walk down with me?" he asked Sara, who appeared happy to trail about after him all day.

"Hey, we brought a picnic," called out Tamsin as they started down towards the collecting ring. "Want to join us at lunchtime?"

Sara waved vigorously and gave a thumbs-up, patting her shoulder-bag to indicate that she too had provisions.

"Let's move about a bit till the race starts - it's freezing!" Emerald pulled her woolly hat down firmly over her ears, and they walked further into the forest where the dogs started happily snuffling about. Emerald was distracted by taking photos on her phone of the bare trees, some ancient and covered with ivy and lichen, when the sound of a shot made them all jump. The shot was followed by cheering and shouting. Emerald put her hand to her heart, "That must be the start of the race! We'd better get over there."

CHAPTER SEVENTEEN

They rushed back through the trees to the track, Tamsin hurriedly clipping all the dogs to their leads.

"Look! They've begun!" Emerald pointed down the hill where a mass of colourful riders were beginning to spin out into a thread, some clearly jostling for position at the front. The cheering and shouting of the crowd followed them up the hill as they rode their course. And there were intermittent whistle-blasts too.

As they crested the hill they had split into two distinct groups. The lead riders raced past in a flurry of metallic noise and speed, their tyres spewing showers of gravel as they turned, making Tamsin gasp and keep the dogs safely behind her. The whistles carried on down the hill as they sped down and the next bunch came whooshing and clattering by.

The riders spread out even more as the laps went on. They spotted Andrew in the second group the first time he went round. Next lap he was further back, and now they couldn't see him at all.

"Hope he hasn't hurt himself .." Emerald shouted anxiously over the noise of the race and the shouts of the crowd further down the hill.

There was a gap while no riders came, then a whistle-blast announced the next group.

"I've worked out what the whistles are for," Tamsin called out. "The steward blows it as a rider or group passes him. Warning to people further down the track I suppose."

"I don't need warning - I'm keeping well away!" laughed Emerald. And they were very glad they were a fair distance from the course, as a new group came through and one rider leapt over a bumpy tree root, twisted in the air, and hurtled off the track to land in a heap below them. They ran down towards him, but the groaning rider was already pulling himself up into a sitting position and rubbing his shins.

"Are you ok?" they both asked.

"Oh, it's Johnny, isn't it?" said Tamsin as Johnny Lightholder pulled off his helmet and tossed it onto the grass in disgust.

"Yes, it's Johnny, and I've just been shoved off the track."

"Really? Someone pushed you? Who?"

"They pushed me alright. Dunno." He rubbed his elbow and winced. "All in black. Couldn't see their number."

"Sure they didn't just skid into you by accident? You were all so close together as you came round the bend out of those trees."

"They did it on purpose. I saw him stick his elbow out. I'll kill him if I catch him …"

"Do you want a hand up?" Emerald spoke soothingly.

"I'll just catch my breath here, thanks. I'll have to wait till the race is over then go down the track."

"There are a good few less racers now," Tamsin looked over to the track where smaller groups hurtled by. "Will we see a procession of wounded riders and broken bikes at the end of the race?"

"Something like that. Here, you were at that dead geezer's memorial, weren't you. I told you people were trying to sabotage us."

Tamsin and Emerald exchanged glances over Johnny's head.

"Johnny, do you think that Ferdinand had anything to do with these accidents?"

"Him? What, the dead bloke? Dunno. Maybe. It all started around that time. Poking his nose into our business. Maybe he was a spy."

"So someone despatched him before he could report back?"

"Here, you're not suggesting one of us did him in? Weren't nothing to do with us. We're peaceable types. Just 'cos we like hurling ourselves about on hillsides at the weekends doesn't mean we go about killing people."

Tamsin held up her hands, "Steady on! Someone definitely did kill him. Just wondering if that could be the reason."

"The police don't seem to have come up with a theory. Mind you, they wouldn't tell us if they had, but ..." Emerald ended lamely.

"You're in with the rozzers are you?" Johnny snorted derisively.

"Shall I ask that steward if he has a first-aid box?" Tamsin tried to change the subject.

"Nah, I'm ok. I'll coast down when the race is over .. which sounds like it's about now," he added as a big cheer went up at the bottom of the hill amongst all the flags. He got up stiffly, brushed himself down and checked over his bike. "Now I'll go and find that bloke in black and ..."

".. have a stern word with him?" interjected Emerald before he could make any more ill-advised threats.

"Yeah. I'll 'have a stern word with him'," he mocked her voice as he mounted his bike and started the downward descent, cautiously.

"I'm going to give the dogs a bit of freedom again. Let's take that path over there and work our way down away from the track."

"What do you think of all that?" asked Emerald, giving Quiz a quick scratch on the top of her head as they started walking again.

"He wasn't very far up in the race. What would be the point of sabotaging him? Surely someone in the front group would be a better target, if any?"

"I think Mr.Lightholder rather fancies himself. So maybe he had to blame someone else for his fall to protect his ego," Emerald observed shrewdly.

"Think you've hit the nail on the head! They were all so bunched together it was impossible to see what happened. I'm still puzzled about that package he was passed on the Hills. Oh, and I wonder what happened to Andrew? We lost him around Lap 3."

By the time they'd walked down through the trees and cut back in towards the bottom of the track near the milling crowd by the finish line, they saw Sara supporting Andrew who was leaning heavily on her.

"Someone pushed him over!" she said breathlessly. "I saw it!"

Tamsin and Emerald glanced at each other in puzzlement.

"Perhaps we maligned Johnny?" Tamsin said quietly, then more loudly, "Are you alright, Andrew? Where are you hurt?"

"It's my knee. And I whacked my shoulder as I landed," he rubbed the offending joint. "I hope it's just bruised, but I certainly won't be doing any more riding today."

"He saw who it was!" Sara said, still fussing over her man.

"Well, I didn't really. It was all too fast. But they were all in black, that I do remember, ow!" he shifted uncomfortably.

"Johnny Lightholder said he was knocked off by someone in black. I thought he was exaggerating, but now .. I guess he was telling the truth!"

"Let's get you to the first-aid tent, wherever that is," said Emerald in an unwonted moment of practicality.

And it was there that they found the loudly complaining Johnny Lightholder being treated. Adam was talking to him urgently. "I wonder if they'll try anything in the Downhill?"

"We'll need to scout ahead of our chaps' runs and make sure there's nothing fishy on the track," said Johnny grimly. "I'll join you in a minute, when this gorgeous nurse has finished with my leg." He gave a leering grin to the nurse who ignored him entirely, packed up her gear and strutted away to the next casualty, of which there seemed an unending stream.

"Think I'll just use your bike for shopping," Emerald said quietly. "Don't fancy all this daredevil stuff!"

"Nor me!" said Tamsin with fervour. "I wonder where we can watch the big race from. I need to get out of this tent now, people are eying the dogs, and it's pretty busy."

"I'm going to take Andrew home," Sara was waiting outside the tent. He's just getting help loading his bike into his car. We'll have to collect that tomorrow - hope he can drive by then."

"We're going to keep our eyes out on the big event," Tamsin told her.

"We're not really any further forward as far as Ferdinand's concerned. But this biking crowd seem to be in ferment!"

"It's a shame. They're mostly so nice .. Ah, here's the walking wounded. Come on Andrew, home with you!" And they left together, Andrew still hobbling and possibly unnecessarily clasping Sara's hand.

Emerald was watching them go, as Tamsin wrapped her scarf round her face and said, "Let's see what we can see!" and started walking up the hill again, leading her ever-patient dogs.

CHAPTER EIGHTEEN

As it turned out, the place Tamsin chose was exactly the wrong place to see the momentous events. They were just beginning to tire of what seemed the never-ending cascade of whistles, scrunching tyres, and whooshing riders, when they heard shouts from the other side of the track.

"What's going on over there?" Emerald stood up on her toes and craned her neck to see. "Everyone's scurrying about just by that wooded area - lots of people whistling."

"Those different whistles must mean 'rider down'. We've had a crash course in mountain bike races today! Forgive the pun ..." Tamsin tilted her head and smiled.

Another whistle-blast reminded them that a rider was on his way so they pulled back from the course. With a staggered start, any number were on the track racing at the same time, getting timed individually.

"We can't cut across - let's go down to the bottom and see what we can find out."

And that's where they'd arrived when they saw a rider being stretchered to a waiting ambulance. Unashamedly they peered at the face just visible over the blanket.

"It's Django!" they chorused.

Adam was fussing round the stretcher as it was being loaded.

"What happened, Adam? Is he going to be ok?"

"Another so-called 'accident'," said Adam through gritted teeth. "This has been a terrible day."

"Have there been other injuries, to people who aren't Nighthawks, I mean?" This from Tamsin.

"The First-Aid tent had plenty of other people in there," prompted Emerald, who was holding the rather cold Moonbeam in her arms.

"There's always bumps and scrapes. But not on this scale, to one group."

"So what happened to Django?"

"Someone put a jagged branch below a jump. Wasn't there before."

"Euuw!" said Emerald, and shuddered.

"Looks as though he may be out of the Worlds," he added gloomily as the ambulance started little darts of its siren to clear the path, and headed out to the road.

"Where is he?" demanded a frantic voice just then. "Where's Django?"

Cynthia was running towards them and Adam reached out to grab her as she looked ready to chase the ambulance. "Here girl, he'll be alright," he soothed her as she fought to get free.

"He's in good hands," Tamsin said, rather helplessly.

The ambulance got to the road and Cynthia suddenly stopped struggling and leant limply against Adam's shoulder. He closed his eyes and sighed.

"Er, we'll pick up the news later .." Emerald said lamely, as she grabbed Tamsin's elbow to steer her and the dogs away.

"So Adam is soft on Cynthia, but Cynthia .."

".. has the hots for Django!"

"Dear, oh dear, what a tangle they're all in. No chance of finding any more about the mysterious Ambrose today. I imagine Majella will not be receptive to questions at the moment. Presumably the women's race is next. Wonder where she is?"

As they moved up the hill a little away from the crowds, they saw the riders gathering near the start flags. A shot from the starter's pistol, much whistling and the noise of cheering moving up the hill with the cyclist indicated that the race had indeed started.

"Honestly? I'm getting pretty bored watching cyclist after cyclist whiz past us," said Emerald, hunching her shoulders in her jacket.

"I get you," Tamsin agreed fervently as they heard a whistle. "Think I've had my fill too - wait, isn't that very tall girl coming down now Majella?"

"Yes, I think you're right .."

As Majella cornered before them they could see her determined face, her jaw set, her eyes flashing. Her hands gripping the handlebars firmly as she hoisted the front of the bike over a tree-root, landed with a skid and sped fast on down the track.

"Look! She's made it to the bottom."

"That was a big cheer that went up - wonder if she did a good time?"

"Can we go now?" asked Emerald plaintively, clutching the woolly-jumpered Moonbeam to her with one arm and blowing on her other gloved hand in a vain and hopeless attempt to warm it.

"Ok, let's head. It's a long tramp up and over that hill." Tamsin eyed the steep ascent and slowly shook her head. "Let's walk down and maybe we'll hear how Majella did. Then we can walk round on the road."

"Oh, thank goodness for that! I'm cold and tired."

"And shocked too?" She reached over and clipped the lead to Moonbeam and put her down on the ground. "Let's walk fast and warm up. We can talk about it at home when Feargal's back from his footie match."

CHAPTER NINETEEN

It was already beginning to get dark when they at last got back to the trusty Top Dogs van. The puddles under their feet were beginning to freeze over, signalling treacherous driving conditions to come. As it happened, by the time they'd made their slow way home to Pippin Lane, slightly warmer as they'd had the van heater on full all the way back from the Forest of Dean, they found a message from Feargal.

Pile-up on the Worcester Road. Got to cover it. I have news - tomorrow teatime at yours?

Tired from the long cold day, Tamsin asked Emerald to text him back while she sorted the dogs' food, "Bit of a relief actually," she said as she got the fire going in the living room. "I think I've had enough peopling for one day!"

The weather was a good bit warmer on Sunday morning, so after a short dog walk in the thin wintry sunshine to shake off sleep (the dogs were still fairly tired from their long day in the Forest), Tamsin settled down to write her monthly piece for the *Malvern Mercury*.

"Fancy me having my own column!" she said as she finished her piece - about how to protect your dog in the cold weather. "Ooh, nearly forgot to add the bit about washing the road salt off their paws ... I'll just do that now," and she frowned at the screen again, her tongue sticking out between her teeth as she worked.

"Is the column doing well for you? In terms of enquiries?"

"It is - it's fantastic! I got two this morning. Along with a weird heavy breathing call."

"Heavy breathing? Yuk!" said Emerald with feeling.

"No, not really heavy breathing. Just nothing. They rang off at the end of my message."

"Perhaps they're very shy?"

"Or didn't like my message, with the dog barking! Never mind. They can ring again. So the column is doing well in getting people to ring, though sometimes they just want more free training - but I'm getting good at steering them into actually paying for a course." She shut the laptop with a flourish. "Perhaps you should do a yoga column? Why not ask Feargal how to get it?"

"Good idea. I could add photos of me doing the poses. Hmm. I'll ask him!"

"Don't turn it into a dodgy 'page 3' column or you'll get the wrong sort of enquiries!" laughed Tamsin, referring to the cheap and nasty tabloid newspapers' infamous girlie photos on page 3.

"I'll do my best," smiled Emerald.

And when Feargal arrived in a flurry of energy and tallness and happy dogs, they were content to snuggle round the fire and eat hot buttered toast and honeycomb as they grilled him for news.

"Lovely honey," said Feargal, licking his fingers.

"Got it from the market in town. It's local. So's this loaf."

"You do well for local food - you always furnish me with something tasty from nearby. I think it's thanks to you I don't have scurvy," he grinned. "I remember all that lovely fruit you got from Bishop's Green."

"Ah, Bishop's Green! The Case of the Mad Archer! I must drop by there again and pick up some more."

Feargal put his plate aside. "Now. I've been talking to our sister papers. I was checking out the names we have. It seems Majella lived in Shropshire for a couple of years."

"Shropshire? Shropshire ... Shropshire ... yes! Charity said the Glossop family came from that direction."

"Maybe there's a connection there?"

"Let me think ... Ferdinand was here looking for Ambrose. According to Cynthia we need to talk to Majella to find out more about him. The Glossop family originated in Shropshire or thereabouts, so maybe Ferdinand and Ambrose were friends in Shropshire .."

"And Majella took up with one of them!" said Feargal.

"And it looks like it was Ambrose," added Emerald.

"We're getting somewhere!" Tamsin jumped up scattering toast crumbs, to the delight of the nearest dog.

"We need to find out what the connection was."

"Yes Em, were they all friends? Business partners? Love triangle ... Feargal, can you dig up anything about Ferdinand and Ambrose in Shropshire? I don't know why it's so hard to find anything out about them. The police have been very quiet - what does your mole have to say?"

"Still on holiday, I'm sorry to say. People can make themselves fairly invisible if they want to - even these days. This makes me think there could be a business venture involved, maybe something a bit shady. I'll have another sniff." He turned to look at the bouncing noises coming from the far end of the living room. "I think it must be getting on for dinnertime in Banjo's mind."

"Yes, he loves to play that game of bouncing and catching his ball when he thinks it's time for his grub!"

"At least he hasn't lost it under the bookcase today."

"So far!" laughed Emerald. "But Moonbeam is at the ready to save the day if she has to - look at her watching him!"

And they smiled to see Moonbeam perched quivering on Tamsin's lap, intently watching Banjo's game and waiting for her moment to shine.

They were interrupted by a tinny barking sound - the ringtone for Tamsin's phone.

"Oh, it's Sara!" she said, answering it where she sat. And after a few enquiries about Andrew - all good and just nursing some bruises, apparently - she learnt that Django was coming out of hospital later today, but wouldn't be riding again for a good while.

"Ligaments, you say, not broken bones? ... Yes, I do believe they can take quite a while. How disappointing for him ... And what of Johnny Lightholder?"

It seemed that Johnny Lightholder was fine but hopping mad and complaining to anyone who would listen.

"I had no idea this sport was so dangerous!" Tamsin said to the others as she ended her call. "We've only been involved a couple of weeks and we already have one dead body, one person in hospital, and two others walking wounded."

"Three, if you count me!" said Feargal, stretching his long legs out to the fire.

"We have to put a stop to it." Emerald said with determination.

"But we have to know who to stop! Do you think the two things are connected? Ferdinand's murder and the sabotage?"

"Good question," said Feargal, reaching for some more of the hot buttered toast Emerald had made during Sara's call. "Thanks Emerald! I'll keep eating this as long as you keep it coming. Maybe we're dealing with two distinct things. I can't quite see how they can be connected."

"It's like that body in the air raid again - I'll explain in a minute," said Tamsin responding to Feargal's puzzled look. "Someone wants us to connect the two. They're using the one to hide the other."

"Gotcha."

"Do you think you can risk your personal safety and talk to Majella?" asked Emerald with a crooked smile.

"On Wednesday night? I think I'll have to. I'll get her on her own somehow - this Shropshire episode is obviously a sore point."

"Think you'll have more info from your spies by then?"

"Hope so. Don't mind if I do ..." he said, as he polished off the last slice of toast.

"At least Majella didn't get injured in the race yesterday," Tamsin stroked Banjo's ear thoughtfully. "I wonder if that means anything?"

"That whoever's doing it doesn't care about the women succeeding?"

"Or that they don't think they will, so they're not a threat?"

"Or," said Emerald, "that Majella is specifically not being targeted ..."

"Yes! And that could mean the sabotagers like her .."

"Or, that she's involved!" Feargal jumped in.

"The plot thickens!" laughed Tamsin. "I've got a busy couple of days of classes and home visits up till Wednesday evening. But we could wander up to *Flying Pedals* again, Emerald, do a bit of noseying round?"

"I can always find something else wrong with the bike. I know just what nuts to loosen ..."

"I have a feeling Howard was trying to shut Brenda up when we were there last time."

"He was very quick to interrupt her when she mentioned Ferdinand's visit, that's true."

"Worth a try?"

"Worth a try!" agreed Feargal, brushing the crumbs off his lap and leaning back in the armchair with a satisfied sigh, patting his tummy with both hands. "Got plans for today? How about finding a film for us to watch?" And the friends put murders out of their mind and enjoyed laughing the rest of the day away watching films together.

Little were they to know what a turn things would soon take!

CHAPTER TWENTY

"Let's go up after lunch - you'll have plenty of time to get to The Cake Stop before your Tuesday class then." said Tamsin as she balanced a little biscuit on Quiz's nose. The dog sat perfectly still, staring cross-eyed at the delicacy, till Tamsin said "Geddit!" whereupon in one swift movement she tossed it up in the air and snapped it with her jaws.

"Good girl," laughed Emerald. "Ok, about 3?"

"I thought we could drive up, save pushing the bike all the way up the hill. Sling it in the back of the van along with your class gear. Shouldn't be too busy in the shop at that time of day, I don't suppose. Then you can take the bike in and cycle home later, or leave it in the van and walk."

"Good plan! Tell me again what Feargal said on the phone this morning. When I'm upside down I can get things out of order."

"Too strange ..." Tamsin eyed her yogi friend. "And you go upside down at the drop of a hat. He said he'd found that Ferdinand and Ambrose were running some kind of business in Shropshire, not sure what. But it failed and Ferdinand was declared bankrupt. And we thought maybe Ferdinand was trying to track Ambrose down to get money off him."

"Wonder what brought him to the Nighthawks?"

"They must both have been involved in cycling, I imagine. Remember they both bought things at the shop together. And he'd have known that Majella came from Malvern. If it's true that she was living with one of them, of course."

Emerald buried her nose in Opal's soft furry neck and breathed the feline scent deeply. "I want to know why Howard was trying to shut Brenda up when she tried to tell us about Ferdinand."

"That's certainly odd ... He was out of the office like a greyhound out of the traps. Speaking of hounds, you can come too, Moonbeam. You look so cute in the bicycle basket." And scooping up the little dog for a kiss, she added, "I'm off out now to a 1 o'clock in Halfkey. I'll be back in time for some grub then we can set off."

So it was later that day when they trundled into *Flying Pedals*, Emerald pushing the bike with Moonbeam perched in the basket.

"Oh dear," said Brenda as the bike bell on the shop door jangled and the three of them processed in, "bike gone wrong again?"

"Ah, it's just this part here," began Emerald, pointing to part of the back wheel. Seems to have come loose. It actually happened just after the memorial on the Hills."

"Oh, I remember, you were the ones who found that unfortunate young man! Did you find out what you wanted about him?"

"Brenda! Would you deal with this phone call please? I'll take over here." Howard had appeared in the doorway, and he put a hand on Brenda's back to chivvy her into the office.

He leant on the counter with both hands, making himself as tall as possible so he could look down at his customers. "Now what can we do for you two ladies?" He gave a smile which was more of a grimace.

"Oh!" said Emerald, as Tamsin lifted Moonbeam out of the basket and held her close. "It's this adjustment here - seems to be slipping .."

"Take it out for Mark to look at, and get him to fix it properly this time. He's - ah - in the shed round the back."

Tamsin and Emerald pushed the bike to the door and looked helpless.

"Left out of the door and round the back. You'll find him there." He turned to the office to close the conversation.

"Well, doesn't that just confirm what we thought?" whispered Tamsin as they walked round the side of the old shop.

"He really doesn't want Ferdinand mentioned, does he!" agreed Emerald. "This must be the shed."

Tamsin peered into the gloom and jumble of old bike parts, calling, "Mark! Mark, are you there?" Getting no answer they both moved into the shed, their eyes adjusting to the dark.

Suddenly they heard the door slam behind them! Tamsin turned and grabbed the handle, but already they could hear the key turning in the old lock.

Emerald whimpered and clung to Tamsin's arm as they heard footsteps leaving.

"Don't worry Em," Tamsin whispered, "we can fix this. Got your phone?"

She nodded dumbly and scrabbled in her pocket.

"Text Feargal first of all. Then have two 9s dialled, ready for the third. Let's see how we can get out of here." Tamsin turned to look around the dark cobwebby old shed. "There must be something we can use to poke the key out."

"The signal's very poor so close under the hill - don't know if this text will send .." Emerald said with a shaky voice, texting with equally shaky fingers. They both started looking for some sort of pointy gadget.

"This is where we could do with a walking pole!"

"I don't like gallows humour," wailed Emerald. "What about this piece of metal?"

"Perfect!" Putting Moonbeam down, Tamsin used the torch on her phone to peer into the lock, poking and prodding at the end of the old-fashioned mortice key. Adding a few grunts and curses, and an ouch or two, eventually they heard a clatter as the big key fell to the ground outside.

Looking through the big gap under the shed door, Tamsin cursed again. "It's only gone and bounced away off a stone! I'll see if I can reach it." With more grunts she got down on the floor and reached her arm out, right up to her shoulder, her fingers stretched out waggling for the key.

"Can't reach it. It's about a yard away," she said, as she stood up and brushed the dirt off her clothes.

"What are we going to do?" Emerald's voice was querulous. "I hate the dark!"

"Panic not! We can do this .." Tamsin started casting about for something longer than her first pointy piece of metal.

"Look at Moonbeam! She's crouched down looking at what you were looking for!"

"Moonbeam! Of course! Moonbeam, go fetch it, girl!"

And Moonbeam, whose nose was sniffing the air vigorously, got down on her side and slithered through the narrow gap.

"It's like she reassembles her bones so she can get under! I always wonder how she can fit under your bookcase." Emerald said, beginning to brighten up.

Tamsin was on her knees again. "Get it, Moonbeam! Pick it up! Over there ..."

As she watched, Moonbeam located the key with her nose, carefully picked it up despite the nasty rusty metal taste, and brought it back to the gap, dangling from one tooth, where she dropped it with a clang.

"Good girl!" enthused Tamsin. "Extra rations for you tonight, you wonder-dog!" and she pulled in the key, put it in the lock and turned it. With a sigh of relief she felt the lock click and the door opened. "Quick! Bring the bike! Let's get out of here!"

And they scurried round the corner of the shop only to bump into Mark.

They stopped dead, mouths open. Then Mark said, "Your friend Feargal just rang me. He said you were stuck in the shed. What happened?"

"What happened indeed!"

"We were locked in."

"Someone shut the door behind us and locked us in!"

Mark gaped at them. "But what were you doing out here? We never use that shed - it's just a dumping-ground."

"Howard sent us there. Told us you were working out there."

Mark's face paled as he got the implication of this. His boss kidnapping his customers!

"Where is he now?"

"He went out - about ten minutes ago. I saw him drive off, fast. Hang on, I hear a car - is this him?"

Emerald and Tamsin shuffled closer together, Moonbeam safely between Tamsin's feet. They heard a door slam and running feet, and Feargal appeared in front of them.

They both sighed with relief and Emerald tried not to cry.

"What on earth's going on?" he demanded.

"Someone locked us in an old shed round the back - must have been Howard."

"Good Lord! What did you do to annoy him?"

"Brenda asked us about Ferdinand. It wasn't even us. He got rid of her, then ... got rid of us."

"So how did you get out?"

"Moonbeam!" said Emerald happily, reaching down to stroke the little dog's head. "Moonbeam got under the door - you know how she finds Banjo's ball for him?"

"I'd managed to poke the key out of the door, but it fell beyond my reach," Tamsin explained.

"And Moonbeam got under and found the key? How did she know to pick it up?"

"It was the only thing on the ground with scent on - so naturally she went for it."

"Amazing. Well done young Moonbeam - your trick saved the day! You both look wrecked. Can you get yourselves home?"

"I've got class at Jean-Philippe's," said a very subdued Emerald.

"It's ok - I'll drop her there. In fact I'll stay there for a while to calm myself down too. Nasty business ... What are you going to do, Feargal?"

"Mark and I will stay here and confront Howard when he comes back. That right, Mark?"

Mark was clearly anxious about his job, but he swallowed hard, straightened up and said, "That's right," nodding firmly.

"Good man. We can't have a kidnapper on the loose. We need a proper explanation, just before we hand him over to the police."

At that moment the shop door opened, its jangly bell ringing, and Brenda peeped out. "Mark? Problem?"

Mark explained the Problem to her, as her face went through several different changes. First with raised eyebrows, then with the colour draining from her cheeks, her mouth falling open in disbelief, and very embarrassed glances at the two women.

"I .. I .. I can't understand it," was all she could say in her anguish.

"These two need to get going and recover," Feargal turned to her. "Can you fix us a cuppa while we wait for your husband?" And he pushed the door open deliberately and he and Mark went in, the flustered Brenda glancing around her anxiously before following them in.

Tamsin turned to Emerald, who was white as a sheet and shaking. "Come on, time for Jean-Philippe's best hot chocolate for us!" and they headed for the van.

CHAPTER TWENTY-ONE

The warmth, the background chatter, the friendly smiles of Jean-Philippe and Kylie, and the feel-good vibe of The Cake Stop - not to mention the hot chocolates with lashings of whipped cream and marshmallows and a big slab of carrot cake to share, which Tamsin wolfed and Emerald pecked at - soon made them both feel better.

Moonbeam was much in demand for cuddles from both of them, and they were feeling ok with the world by the time Shirley arrived early for class, laden with shopping bags as well as her yoga gear. She waved coyly at them from the door, and when invited over to join them she bustled over, weaving between the chairs.

Kylie saw her struggling across and called out to her to confirm her usual Latte. "Yes please, dear," she said, pulling off her gloves and unwinding the scarf from her neck as she sat down with a flump, cold air coming off her.

"And how are you two today? Ooh, hallo Moonbeam - what a pretty little thing you are!"

"We owe your Mark a debt of gratitude," said Tamsin, removing the wagging tail from her face.

"Oh?" Shirley beamed with pride at her miscreant son coming good at last.

"He was coming to our rescue - but in fact Moonbeam had already rescued us!"

"Rescue? Rescue from where?"

"Rescue from *whom*," Emerald leant forward and spoke confidentially. "We were locked in a black shed at the bike shop."

"No! Whoever did that? Maybe the wind blew the door shut."

"The wind didn't send us out to an unused shed to see Mark."

"Nor did the wind turn the key then walk away."

Shirley's mouth was making a perfect O. "Then who ..?"

"It seems," said Tamsin clearly, "that it was Howard."

"That awful man! I wouldn't give him the time of day if it weren't for the fact that Mark is doing his Work Experience with him," she snorted, causing her double chin to wobble alarmingly.

"Why do you say that?"

"He's a bully, that's why. Thinks he's God's gift too. They do say that he has a go at any likely female customers ..."

"He didn't 'have a go' at us," said Emerald, leaning back and crossing her arms.

"Saw that he'd met his match, I expect!" grinned Shirley. "Perhaps your reputation goes before you, Tamsin."

"He locked us in the shed. Who knows when we'd have been found. We sent a text to Feargal which fortunately got through, and he got hold of Mark and told him."

Seeing the surprise on Shirley's face, Tamsin added, "Feargal trusted Mark, you see. And Mark repaid his trust. People do! He was on his way to rescue us, but clever Moonbeam had got us out already."

"Thank Heavens," said Emerald fervently, giving an involuntary shudder, as she noticed tears welling in Shirley's eyes.

"We didn't know whether the text had sent, so we had to do it ourselves."

"So, er, how did this little dog rescue you?" Shirley wiped her eyes, but was looking a bit doubtful.

"Oh, she crawled under the gap in the door and found the key we'd knocked out of the lock."

"How clever!" Shirley clapped her hands together in a quite unprecedented show of excitement and smiled fondly at Moonbeam. "But why on earth did Howard lock you in?"

"We'd love to know, but we *think* it was because Brenda wanted to talk about Ferdinand - you know, the guy who was killed."

"He keeps Brenda well under his thumb. Don't know why she puts up with it, especially with all the womanising."

"So who does he 'womanise' with? Anyone we know?"

"He likes the fit ones. Part of the reason he runs a bike shop, I suppose. And he likes a bit of glam. I hear that one of the Nighthawks girls is doing very well and likely to win medals and things. I'll bet he's going after her! Oh, thank you Kylie!" she handed Kylie her card and focussed on her latte which had just arrived.

"So ..." Tamsin was thinking aloud, "That would be Majella. So .. he thinks Ferdinand had something to do with her, and doesn't want any mention of him?"

"Or Ambrose?" Emerald licked a little cream cheese icing off her fingers before offering her hand to Moonbeam to finish the job.

"Or Ambrose. Are you thinking what I'm thinking, Emerald?"

"That Howard has a thing for Majella, and knows she was tied up with Ferdinand and Ambrose, and didn't like the fact that they seemed to be turning up in her life again?"

"I suppose his bullying is a way of controlling everyone."

"Jason certainly looks browbeaten."

"And very resentful. He clearly doesn't like his father. That's the trouble with bullying. One day you go just too far, and everything blows up in your face. Hey, you don't think my heavy breather is one of these guys, do you?"

"You still getting silent phone calls?"

"Yes. Always withheld number. There've been four so far."

"Weird."

"But I must suggest something to Feargal right now .." Tamsin turned to her phone and buzzed a text to Feargal: *Ask Howard about Majella*.

"So maybe," Shirley joined in again, "maybe he thinks that he can control who Majella sees, and .. and what? She'd be half his age. Perhaps he lives in a fantasy world."

"If he thinks kidnapping is a way to shut people up, he must do! Oh look, here's the rest of the gang arriving," Emerald waved to her students as they filed in and headed towards their table. "Let's change the subject."

"But do tell Mark how grateful we are for his efforts to rescue us!" Tamsin got up, "C'mon Moonbeam, let's get out of here before they have you standing on your head or your tail or something! Got all your gear, Em? See you later!"

And as she passed the other students, some of whom were her own students as well, and nearly all the rest she knew from the time when Emerald's whole class had got caught up in a dramatic murder, she waved cheerily and left the café.

And once home she occupied her mind with sunnier thoughts than being locked in dirty dark sheds. She played some games with the dogs and fed them and Opal. By the time Emerald arrived home she was feeling peckish again and beginning to bang saucepans around.

"You're back early - everything ok?" she said as she looked at her friend through the steam.

"Andrew gave me a lift home. He could see I was exhausted. That episode really took it out of me," she said, dropping into a chair. "Anyway it was beginning to rain again, so he didn't mention that I looked wrecked."

"Darling, you never look wrecked!"

Emerald stifled a yawn and leant on the table. "But you know, I asked Andrew about Howard. You know he's been keen on biking of one sort or another for years, any sport and Andrew's your man!"

"And?"

"He said that fits. The Majella thing. He's seen Howard go all soppy over her before. Bit proprietorial, you know."

"Hmm. Perhaps he's nuts. Been inhaling bicycle lubricant for so long it's affected his brain."

"But shouldn't we report him to the police, all the same?"

"I think we can get him another way," said Tamsin slowly. "An idea is growing in the back of my mind. Let's leave it there for now and have some grub. Animals are all fed, so have a snuggle with Opal till I've got supper ready. We need a bit of pampering!"

CHAPTER TWENTY-TWO

Tamsin woke the next day with that strange sensation of suddenly remembering something ghastly. Her stomach sank as she remembered her fear when she was trapped in the black shed. She had stayed strong for Emerald, but she was very glad she hadn't been on her own. So as she got up she gave Moonbeam a special kiss and hug.

"There, Banjo - your crazy game saved us!" and she laid her hand on the puzzled dog's back and threw him the nearest toy. He was happy to take it, shaking it and tossing it in the air and catching it again, his eyes sparkling and his beautiful tail swishing.

After a comforting breakfast and plenty of coffee, she got a text from Feargal.

Got info. You in today?

Got a 3 and a 4.30, she texted back. *Lunch?*

In reply to this she got a series of symbols and little images which she took to mean yes.

"Where's Emerald?" was the first thing Feargal asked when the dogs had finished mobbing him.

"She's gone to the Buddhist Temple for some meditation. She needs a break from all this, so it's you and me for now."

"Poor girl. Nasty business. But I think Howard realised he'd gone a step too far, and he's got his come-uppance."

"Tell all!" Tamsin furnished him with a plate and mug and put a dish of sandwiches and salad on the table, along with the coffee pot and cream jug.

"We were sitting in the shop drinking tea when he came back - that's Brenda, Mark and me. He looked a bit surprised, especially when Brenda said 'I think you should sit down and listen, Howard'. He hesitated, then realised he had no way out, so he sat. I'd decided I was going to go full-on with him. So I told him that I was going to get *Flying Pedals* closed down. You should have seen his face! He spluttered, and was going to argue back till Brenda told him he had to stop bullying people and listen. I explained that an article in the *Malvern Mercury* about what he'd just done would be enough to finish him. He began to get frantic - a bit pathetic really. He pleaded with me, complained about libel. I had to point out that if it was the truth it was not libel, and there were witnesses prepared to come forward. Brenda, bless her, really came into her own. She told him she'd put up with it all for years and she was putting up with it no longer. That there was no fool like an old fool, and so on. 'I want you to get help,' she said, as her final word."

"I'm eating all the sandwiches," Tamsin said, pushing the plate towards him. "Pause to eat!"

And after a break for sustenance, Feargal carried on his tale. "Howard was more afraid of Brenda by this stage than of me. So he assured her he would go to counselling. 'But I'm not a sex fiend!' he protested. He said he had only a fatherly interest in Majella, and always had done, since she first started winning bike races as a child. He had his son Jason, and supposed that he adopted Majella as a kind of daughter. He missed her when she went to live in Shropshire for a couple of years and was off the Malvern racing scene, and he knew that she had come back broken-hearted. She wouldn't speak about it. And all he knew was that it involved a man called Ambrose."

"Ah! So when this new guy Ferdinand showed up and started asking questions about Ambrose, he wanted to stamp it out."

"Right. I asked him point-blank whether he had killed Ferdinand. He was utterly shocked. He said he didn't know he was on the Hills that night, and moreover, neither was he, as they'd been at a family New Year's Eve party in Oxfordshire. Brenda assured me that was so. I have to say I believed her."

"Did you find out why he locked us in?"

"I asked him that too. 'Why did you kidnap the two women?' He broke down at that stage. Just kept saying, 'I don't know, I don't know'."

"He needs that help. Does Brenda know where to send him?"

"I've promised to send her a list that we have at the *Mercury*. HR are ready to stamp out bullying at a stroke, and sometimes they have to deal with major meltdowns, so they are armed with resources! He's going to have to go along with it now. There were three witnesses."

"And what did Mark make of all this?"

"Mark actually surprised me. You know how you always say that if you set a dog a difficult task he'll try hard to complete it? Well, Mark's like that. I think for so long he's been caught up with the wrong crowd, and labelled as a wrong'un, that he really blossoms when he's given responsibility. He didn't crow over his boss's crisis. He was very supportive, and promised to help Brenda whenever Howard was at a session."

"His mother's a good sort. I suppose 'blood will out'. All very interesting. And sad. But I think we need to talk to Majella and find out what's what. And - whether it had anything to do with Ferdinand's murder."

"Tonight! It's bike night on the Hills tonight. Wanna come?"

"As long as I don't have to ride any bikes, sure!" And so they arranged where and when to meet.

"Be sure to wrap up well. I'll be keeping warm pedalling. It's windy today, the wind'll cut you in half up there on top of the Beacon."

"Thanks for the encouragement. You won't recognise me. I'll look like the Michelin Man. I'm well used to keeping warm in the elements. I won't bring any dogs for once. Too dangerous in the dark - don't want them hit by a flying bike."

"I wonder if we're getting any closer?" mused Feargal as he put on his padded jacket and rammed his fleece hat down over his unruly red curls.

"We're certainly finding out a few home truths about the Nighthawks! But I don't know if we're getting closer ... Will you be able to find out any more about the business venture Ferdinand and Ambrose were involved in?"

"I'm waiting for some responses to come back. I'll keep hunting."

"Goodness, look at the time! I must fly." And they both headed out to their vehicles to go about their lawful occasions.

CHAPTER TWENTY-THREE

They met as agreed, Feargal on his bike, kitted out in helmet, gloves, and the works. Tamsin, as threatened, was wrapped from top to toe in many layers, a rainbow-striped scarf wrapped around her face, all topped off with a bright pink bobble hat.

And as they plodded up the Hills, mercifully not icy tonight, to the start-point, they were overtaken by some of the Nighthawks, cycling up.

"How do they do it?" demanded Tamsin. "How do they cycle uphill over this rough terrain?"

"Lots of low gears," answered Feargal. "And amazing stamina."

"Stamina. Fitness. Strength." Tamsin paused to catch her breath, watching the mist stream from her mouth as she spoke. "I guess stamping a walking pole into someone requires strength. Though the strongest man in the world couldn't do it unless .."

"Unless they were nuts, or really, *really*, hated the victim," Feargal finished for her.

Tamsin shivered. "Or feared him. Hope not nuts, or who knows who may be next on the list."

When they arrived at the gathering point, Jim said a few words then handed over to Django who was running the night's session. His arm was in a sling, so clearly not able to race, but wild horses wouldn't have kept him away - never mind wild cyclists! He outlined the course they would be taking, keenly listened to by all, and emphasised safety and respect for other riders and hill-users - at which most of the cyclists switched off and started fiddling with their bikes or catching the eye of friends. Clearly they'd heard this speech before.

Feargal, pushing his bike with Tamsin in tow, drifted over to where Majella and Cynthia were getting their bikes prepped, and asked outright, "Did you hear what happened yesterday, at *Flying Pedals?*"

"No?" responded Majella, straightening up. "Is it something I should know about?"

Feargal stepped a bit closer, his bike blocking Cynthia, who took the hint and moved off. "It's something that may concern you."

Majella looked startled. "Go on, then," she said flatly, pressing her lips together.

"I believe you met Tamsin before?"

Tamsin obligingly peeled the scarf from her face, and Majella nodded. "You were involved in that murder."

"Well, I wouldn't say 'involved' exactly .." Tamsin began, but Feargal jumped in. "Did you know Howard has a longstanding and abiding interest in you and your welfare?"

Majella blushed. "Howard? He's always supported me, encouraged me with little additions for my bikes - ever since I was a kid."

"Don't you think this was a little strange?"

"No, I never felt there was anything .. odd, or wrong about it. I saw it more as a kind of sponsorship. Nothing inappropriate, you know?"

"That's not how he sees it, unfortunately. He's in a lot deeper than that."

Majella opened her mouth and shut it again. Then said, "So what happened at the shop yesterday that concerns me?"

"Howard overheard Brenda mentioning one Ambrose to Tamsin and her friend,"

"And dog," corrected Tamsin, noting Majella's tight expression at the mention of Ambrose.

"And dog," added Feargal as Majella raised her eyes heavenwards. "Actually the dog is important. Howard sent them out to an unused shed round the back and locked them in."

Majella looked suitably aghast.

"But owing to their ingenuity -"

"- and the dog," added Tamsin.

"And the dog, they got out and got help."

"So? I still don't know .."

"I want to explain to you. Howard is, er, a bit mixed up, shall we say. Obsessively so. He thought by kidnapping Tamsin and her friend - and her dog," he said quickly before Tamsin could butt in again, "he was in some way protecting you."

"It seems he thought that mention of Ambrose or Ferdinand would greatly upset you, and he wanted to spare you," Tamsin softened the blow a bit.

Majella's shoulders slumped, as the last of the bikes set off on the staggered start down the Hill. "You coming, Majella?" someone called out.

"In a minute!" she called back with a false smile, then turned back to her interrogators. "What an eejit he is," she said finally. "I was .. involved with Ambrose for a while, that's all. He upped and left. End of story."

"Is it? The end of the story? Sounds more like the beginning to me."

The first cyclists were already coming up the hill again from their circuit. Adam had been lead bike and he looked towards Majella, leaning on his handlebars while he regained his breath. "You alright Majella?" he asked, looking curiously at Feargal and Tamsin.

"Just setting off thanks Adam," she called back. Then mounting her bike, she snorted, "It's most definitely the end, as far as I'm concerned. And now, if you don't mind, I'm here to practice, not to gossip."

"Ouch!" said Tamsin quietly, as Majella stood up on the pedals and set off at speed. "You'd better go too, hadn't you, Feargal?"

"I will. So the Ambrose secret is revealed."

"Partially revealed. We still don't know why Ferdinand was asking after him. Oh look," she said, as a group of puffed-out cyclists arrived back at the start point. "Cynthia is looking daggers at us. I wonder what she really knows?"

"I'll wait a minute adjusting my bike, then set off before her when she does her second run. May get a chance to find out."

And amidst the scrunching of tyres on gravel, and the subdued shouts of the riders, he made his way across to the start.

A tap on the shoulder had Tamsin spinning round to see who it was. "Django!"

"Got a problem?" he asked coolly, his bandaged arm in a sling across his chest.

"Ah, no, not at all," she smiled brightly. "So glad to see you up and about again! That was a nasty accident." Django nodded in reply, waiting for more. "No," said Tamsin, "there was just something a bit strange at the bike shop yesterday, and we thought Majella may be able to help. But no worries! It's all ok!" and she hurried over to where Adam was standing with Johnny Lightholder.

"You still sniffing around?" Johnny said bluntly. Clearly the Nighthawks were closing ranks against outsiders. There was a definite hostility in the air.

"I enjoyed the race last week so I thought I'd come up to support Feargal as he's just starting out. He was at the memorial - and I bumped into him afterwards." More smiles, in the hope of easing the situation slightly. "Are you better now? That was quite a whack you took."

"Still a bit stiff," he said, drawing himself upright from leaning on his handlebars. As Tamsin suspected, Johnny was very happy to talk about himself, "Bruised ribs and a painful elbow and shoulder - but not much stops me! Fortunately didn't get my collar bone. I vaulted over the handlebars and rolled."

"Learning how to fall is essential to keep yourself intact," said Adam.

"I guess that goes for the whole of life!" Tamsin laughed, thinking of the number of times she'd picked herself up from some disaster and moved on. "Did you find out any more about the accidents?"

Adam stroked his chin and shook his head sadly. "Reckon it's that lot from the Cavaliers."

"The Cavaliers?"

"Yeah, they're a club over in Oxfordshire. Their main rider is a weaselly fellow called Mike. Reckon it's them. We've beaten them in the club standings the last three years."

"Sure to be," said Johnny. "But we don't have any actual proof."

"Can you police the course somehow?"

"We should be able to make sure there are no more obstacles put on the course. But we can't stop deliberate shoving or tripping."

"Hey if you want to be useful, you could keep an eye on the track on the next event. We can't be everywhere."

"Oh yes!" Tamsin realised this was a chance to redeem herself in their eyes. "When's the next event?"

They gave her the details. It was right down at the bottom of Gloucestershire towards Bristol in six weeks' time. Tamsin enthused and took down the info, all the while fervently hoping that the mystery would be solved long since and she'd never have to go near a mountain bike again as long as she lived.

Johnny and Adam took off again down the hill - do they never run out of energy? she wondered - and Feargal came trudging up the path, pushing his bike.

"Uh-oh! What happened to you?"

"I'm fine, but the bike isn't. Hit a rock and buckled the front wheel - look!"

They looked sadly at the damaged bike. "*Let's went, Cisco,*" said Tamsin.

"Let's what?"

"Sorry - family expression my mother used to use. Came from some tv show long, long ago."

"And it means Let's go?"

She nodded.

"You're on. It's too cold to stand about here any longer."

"You're telling me! I've been stamping and bouncing and running on the spot to keep warm. Let's make our goodbyes and go."

It wasn't until they were well on their way back down the hill that Feargal started telling her about what had happened on his run.

"It wasn't intentional!" he protested when she admired his determination to pursue the story, come what may. "It really was an accident. I'd planned on intercepting her at some stage, but not like that."

"I'll believe you, though thousands wouldn't!" she laughed.

"Well, I was sprawled across the track so Cynthia kinda had to stop. She was very nice, checking me over for injuries first of all and asking me some questions to see if I'd banged my head, then a quick look at the bike. She said it just needs a new front wheel and some adjustments. 'Looks like a job for Mark,' I said. Then I grabbed the chance to ask if she'd heard about the carry-on at *Flying Pedals* yesterday."

"Mind this dip here," Tamsin didn't want another crash.

"Thanks. She hadn't, so I told her. She was silent for a bit, then she said, 'So you know about Ambrose now. Majella just said she told you. Satisfied?'"

"Ouch, again."

"Quite. Pretty frosty. So I said to her, 'Not really. It still doesn't tell me what the connection with Ferdinand is.'"

Tamsin turned to face her friend: "And? What did Cynthia say to that?"

"Nothing whatever. She got on her bike and rode off."

"Too weird. And I found them all closing ranks against me, too. Felt very chilly up there, and not just from the wind. You know what?" They'd arrived at the Top Dogs van and Feargal loaded the battered bike in the back just behind the dog crates. "We've actually got somewhere."

"You think?" he backed out of the van and wiped his hands on his trousers.

"I do think. They know there's a connection and it's like getting blood out of a stone finding out what it is. We're clearly onto something." She got into the van and started it, "Let's get this heater going. It may just start warming up before we get home!" And as they turned and started down the hill she added, "Anyway, perhaps you can find out more from your research. We're close!"

"And cold. Hot chocolate before I go?"

"Sure. And Emerald will be home, so we needn't mention all this, ok?" And the friends gave each other a conspiratorial smile.

CHAPTER TWENTY-FOUR

It was Friday before Feargal came back with his newly-discovered information. A Friday which had dawned mercifully warmer than the last two weeks. Warmer, but wet, as the view of the Hills from Tamsin's bedroom window was blurred into looming dark shapes with the streaming rain. They were paying for the extra degrees with rainfall. So in answer to Feargal's text about where and when to meet to debrief, Tamsin happily replied, *Puppy Class at 3, Cake Stop at 11? Who would you like to see?*

Banjo! came the swift reply. *11 it is.*

"Banjo? You up for an outing? We can bring your frisbug!"

Banjo's ears stood up with delight at the word as he wiggled towards her. "Shh, don't tell the others," she smiled.

So shortly before eleven Tamsin was peeling off her wet coat and hat and giving Banjo a rub down with the towel she'd brought with her in her doggy bag. And settling her four-legged friend on his mat with something to chew she started to tuck into her cake while she waited for her two-legged chum.

"Whatcha got there?" asked Feargal as he came and joined her.

"The Furies' Finest! Plain and simple Coffee Walnut today - can't fail with that. What are you having?"

"Just ordered a bacon roll. Let's wait for Kylie to do her magic before we get started. So," he said, leaning back in the armchair and crossing his legs, "You've started your classes up again?"

"Yep," Tamsin swallowed a mouthful of creamy walnutty deliciousness, "Puppy Class starts today. Love Puppy Class! I never tire of all those sweet fluffy gentle little creatures with their wide eyes and their open souls," she smiled, and turned to see Kylie bearing down on them with a bacon roll and mug of coffee. As a concession to the season, the pink-haired barista was wearing thick woolly tights under her tiny ra-ra skirt.

"Hello you two!" she said cheerily. "Hatching a new plot?" she raised an eyebrow.

"No, we're the good guys," laughed Tamsin, "We un-hatch other people's plots!"

"With you on our side we can all sleep peacefully in our beds at night. How's Emerald this weather?"

"She's great thanks! Busy teaching people how to relax and reconnect with their bodies today."

Kylie smiled and flipped her tea-towel over her shoulder before returning to the counter to serve more customers.

After Feargal had demolished his bacon roll in less than a minute, like a one-man pack of ravening wolves, he said, "Here Banjo, have some crumbs from the rich man's table," and passed him a small piece of bacon that he'd reserved specially. Banjo took it very gently in his front teeth, and turned round and lay down on his mat to savour it.

"Well?" asked Tamsin.

"I've got the tie-up between Ferdinand and Ambrose!"

"How did you find out?"

"Not telling you how I know," he said, folding his arms dramatically across his chest, "but I just do."

"Ok Mr.Smugface, spill the beans."

"They were in business together, as we know. And it seems that

Ferdinand had put up most of the money to get started. Ambrose was bringing the expertise."

"If it was business expertise it clearly wasn't worth much."

"That would be true. But it was market knowledge apparently. It was some sort of online shoe business, and Ambrose had been in shoe sales for years."

"So Ambrose was the knowledge, and Ferdinand was the money."

"That's it. And when they went bankrupt there was no money to be found. So my guess is that Ambrose legged it - as we've heard from Majella - with the remaining funds and stock, and Ferdinand had presumably decided it was time to get his money back."

"And that's why he came hunting, following the cycling-and-Majella trail," Tamsin nodded, understanding coming at last.

"And when Howard heard him talking about Ambrose, he didn't like the idea of this connection with his protégée. He was afraid of the relationship with Ambrose being rekindled, and that Majella would move away again and stop racing."

"He panicked. And he doesn't seem to think very much."

"Poor Howard."

"'*Poor Howard*'? Had you forgotten what he did to me and Emerald?"

"Course not - that was awful. And absurd. I mean 'poor Howard' for getting himself into such a state. It's not rational. He's departed from reality somewhere along the line."

"You're right. I should be sorry for him. But I'd really rather he kept his crazy impulses under control. I don't think he had any idea what he was going to do with us."

"That's probably why he fled."

"I think, you know, that we could delve a little deeper into the Howard angle."

"I think you're right. There's more there than meets the eye." Feargal took a swig of his coffee. "Aaaah, delicious."

"And I think as Brenda is the actual brains in that family, we ought to address both of them. Check out this alibi for New Year's Eve. Very easy to say 'Oh, we were visiting friends'. How are you fixed tomorrow?"

They arranged a time to meet at *Flying Pedals,* and Tamsin was careful to make it coincide with Sara's lunch break so they could enjoy a coffee and chinwag together after.

"Tell you what - we need to investigate Jim too. Something definitely not right there. What do you think?"

"It's money again, isn't it. Filthy lucre."

"Mammon. I'm glad I'm not motivated by money. Never have been. So long as I have enough to look after this crowd," she nodded to Banjo peacefully dozing on his mat after his wet frisbee games, "I'm happy."

"And I'm never going to hit the high life doing what I do," added Feargal. "But hey - I love what I do!"

"No ambitions to hit Fleet Street?"

"And spend my time dealing with shady politicians and grubby businesses? Actually I can do all that here, only on a smaller scale. More personal, you know?"

"We have our priorities right. And yet so many get caught out over .. money. Have you found out any more about Jim's business?"

"It appears squeaky clean on the surface. He's into all these worthy organisations - not just the Nighthawks, but he's in the local chamber of commerce, well respected, you know the sort of thing."

"And meanwhile he's fiddling the books."

"Well, we don't *know* that."

"But we're sure going to find out! Maybe he's been gambling the firm's money away, or the bike club's money."

"I don't see him in a cloth cap at the races. But he could be gambling on the stock exchange. Using money from wherever he can access it, then unable to pay it back in the time allowed ... "

"Oh yeah you can kind of gamble on the never-never with stocks, can't you?"

"That's it. You have a few days to cough up if you've committed yourself and your gamble failed. Lots of suicides can happen in those few days, it seems."

"How horrid. We don't want that. But if he's gambling away the club's money, how does that tie up with Ferdinand's murder?"

"I can't see that it does. But you never know. Maybe looking for Ambrose was a red herring. Maybe Ferdinand came to blackmail Jim. He did live in the same general area. Stourport's not that far from Shropshire."

"Maybe he knew something incriminating?"

"Maybe Jim did Ferdinand's company books?"

"Now that I hadn't thought of!" Tamsin leant over and twirled Banjo's ear to soothe herself. And him. Some dogs hate their ears being messed with, but Banjo enjoyed it and tilted his head to press into her hand. "I think we need to check what he was actually up to on New Year's Eve. Maybe he and Gillian were spending the evening at home. But he could have been up there on the Hills dancing a jig in the nude for anybody would notice him. Everyone was paying attention to the fireworks and it was cold. They were wearing hats and scarves and balaclavas and had their hoods up. Very easy to stay hidden."

"We certainly need to check it out."

"We keep uncovering more stuff. First there's Ferdinand, stabbed with a walking pole while cycling incognito on New Year's Eve."

"Then we have the saboteurs from who-knows-where."

"There's Jim's possible misappropriation of funds - or at the very least, tardiness in discharging his duties with the club's money."

"Then there's Howard, raving over Majella."

"Jason dislikes his father." Tamsin said thoughtfully.

"Perhaps he knew what happened before when Majella left and, knowing his father's obsessional, he didn't want trouble starting again."

"Maybe Django's really keen on Majella."

"And he doesn't want a blast from the past?"

"Oh, and let's not forget the mysterious parcel slipped to Johnny Lightholder surreptitiously. What can have been in it?"

"Drugs, I imagine. But then he'd get disqualified. I don't know."

"So what was in the package?" demanded Tamsin.

"Who's trying to wipe out the Nighthawks?" echoed Feargal.

"What's going on with Jim?"

"Why is Howard obsessed?"

"Why was Ferdinand there?"

"And why was he killed?"

Tamsin threw her hands in the air, narrowly missing Kylie who was walking behind her with a tray of coffees, clapped her hand to her mouth, and said to Feargal, "I'm off. See you tomorrow. Lots to think about ..."

CHAPTER TWENTY-FIVE

When Tamsin arrived at the front door of the bike shop late the next morning she was surprised to be clasped by the hand by Verena. Verena had been her first client in the close-knit village of Bishop's Green, where Tamsin had helped resolve a long-standing village difficulty, and she was a firm fan, as well as being friendly with Sara.

"My dear, I've just heard! I simply *knew* you'd be in the thick of it, Tamsin. You're an *excitement* magnet."

"Goodness Verena - lovely to see you! But what are you doing here?"

"I had some errands to run in Malvern and with this weather being so unpredictable I offered Sara a lift. Save her cycling, you know? The roads can be treacherous at this time of year," she sighed theatrically.

Tamsin smiled and nodded and extracted her hand from Verena's grip, giving it a surreptitious shake to restore the blood-flow. "How very kind of you. And how is the delightful little Bingo?"

"Oh, not so little now. He's getting quite grown up. He has such a cute expression with those terrier ears! You simply must come and have another session with him - you work such magic!"

"Love to. Give me a ring at home when I have my diary to hand and we'll fix something."

"Will do! Now I must fly! - got so much to do. That new reclaimed architecture place - want to get some animal statues for the garden. I've rather taken a shine to the Major's deer and hare archery targets, peeping out from the bushes, you know! - see you later, Sara, byeee!"

And out whooshed the indefatigable Verena. Sara was peeling off her gloves. "Who have you come to see? I'm guessing you're not buying a bike?" she grinned.

"Too right. Watching them all trying to kill themselves last week would put any sensible person off! Actually, I'm meeting Feargal here. We want to have a word with Brenda and Howard. Are they about, do you know?"

"I can see them in the office, yeah."

"And here, bang on time, is Feargal! Hi there - let's go in."

Feargal pulled off his woolly hat and ran his fingers through his hair, getting it nice and floppy again. "Howdy," he answered.

Brenda was doing some tidying at the counter when she looked up and saw Feargal, and she paled. "Here again? What can we do for you now?"

"Hi Brenda," Tamsin attempted to relax the atmosphere. "We wondered if we could have a quick word with you both, about New Year's Eve."

As expected, Brenda stiffened. And she turned and led them into the office. "Sara, can you mind the shop please?" Sara nodded and picked up a cloth to start polishing the bikes as Brenda quietly closed the door.

There were two chairs and a stool in the office. Feargal motioned the ladies to take the chairs and Howard to sit on the stool. He himself remained standing, to gain the advantage.

"Now, I think we should be straight with each other," Feargal began. "When I was here last time I indicated what a slender thread your business is hanging on."

"You threatened me, you mean!" Howard blustered.

"I indicated that the two women were entitled to report you for what you did, and that naturally the local press would take an interest, especially if it got to court. So let's stop beating about the bush, Howard. You're not in a position to bargain."

There was a silence while Howard wrung his hands together and stared at the floor. Eventually he straightened up and said, "So what do you want today? Are you trying to blackmail me?" He stuck his round chin out.

"Of course not!" Tamsin spoke up. "We were wondering where you were on New Year's Eve. You told Feargal you were at a friend's party in Oxfordshire. How true is that?"

There was another pause and then Brenda sighed and said, "You may as well know."

Feargal and Tamsin turned to look at her, while Howard studied the floor again.

"I went to my sister's early, in the afternoon, along with Jason. He gets on well with his cousins. They had a fireworks show, then after supper we saw in the New Year. It was too icy to drive by then, so I asked my sister if I could stay the night. I hate driving in the ice at night. So I helped her clear up the next morning and arrived back in Malvern after lunch. It was a bank holiday of course, on New Year's Day, so there was no shop to attend to."

"What about Jason?"

"Jason wanted to get back, so he went back with his father that night. You see, Howard doesn't like fireworks, so he stayed working late on the accounts and whatnot. He got to us around 9, in time for supper. So he was able to take Jason home that night."

Howard looked stricken as all eyes were on him.

"Why did you tell us different, Howard?"

"I .. I .. I thought it would be better. I never went up the Hills that night! As Brenda says, I hate fireworks - the bangs do funny things to my ears. I could hear the display from the office here - that was bad enough."

"You've already lied about that night," Feargal said. "How do we know you aren't lying again now?"

Howard looked about him frantically, like a trapped animal.

"Won't the work you were doing on the computer be time-stamped in some way? Can you show us what you were doing?"

Howard gulped, and with a shaking hand tried to fire up the computer. "Can you get Sara in, Brenda? She usually does the accounts, you see," he turned to Feargal. "She's probably been at them loads since then, and it won't show anything," he laughed nervously.

"Try it." Feargal said grimly. "What accounts were you working on? Tell us now before Sara comes in."

"Um, ah, it was the spare parts and accessories I was working on. Yes. For December. That was it." His glasses had slipped down his sweating nose and he anxiously pushed them up again.

Sara stepped gingerly into the tense atmosphere of the small office, chilly except for the small blower heater under the desk. "What would you like me to look up, Howard?"

When he told her, she said, "Oh those - I was working on them last week, during the break. I think it should show the date of my entries." She clattered on the keyboard and wiggled the mouse about. "Here. Just what I did last week. Nothing before then since mid-December. Is that what you wanted to know?"

They all turned to stare at Howard, who was bent over, silent.

"Thank you Sara," Brenda said quietly, and ushered her from the room.

And they all waited.

Brenda reached over and touched Howard's knee, encouragingly.

He looked up with a surly expression. "I wasn't up the Hills. That's all I'm telling you."

CHAPTER TWENTY-SIX

"I think you need to clarify your position before Chief Inspector Hawkins comes knocking," was Feargal's parting shot, and they left the bike shop. But not before Tamsin arranged to meet Sara in The Cake Stop at her lunch break.

And it was there that she and Feargal arranged to meet after they'd both attended to some other private business in town. Tamsin had some shopping to do and who knew what Feargal was scurrying off to!

"Well, what do you make of all that?" she asked her friend as he brought the coffees over to the table.

"I think there isn't a single person involved in all this who isn't lying, that's what I think," he said as he unloaded the tray and sat down opposite her.

"Extraordinary! Howard is certainly in a mess. I would love to be a fly on the wall right now. I bet Brenda is taking him apart."

"Perhaps she knows what he was really up to."

"Yeah, perhaps he has some secret vice that no-one's meant to know about."

"I think Brenda will sort him out. She seems a good sort. She's probably had to put up with a lot to keep that family together down the years."

"Hey, Jean-Philippe!" said Feargal, looking over Tamsin's head at the approaching figure.

"*Bonjour, mes amis,*" the proprietor said. "No dog today, Tamsin? And no more dramas?"

"No more dramas," she assured her friend. "And just occasionally, very very occasionally, I'm allowed out without a dog. Though it's true, I do feel undressed without one!"

"You have an air about you, you two. I think you're closing in on our murderer, *hein?*"

"Does it show?" smiled Feargal. "You're right, things are becoming clearer."

"Although," interrupted Tamsin, "there are other things that are getting much more confusing! But yes, it's gradually beginning to unravel."

"And this is a friend of yours, *n'est-ce pas?*" The black-haired barista nodded towards the doorway, where Sara stood peering into the café.

"Over here!" Tamsin waved, and Sara hurried over to join them.

"I have an illustrated talk to cover," said Feargal, standing up and drinking the last of his coffee. "An illustrated talk about volcanic activity by our local explorer, would you believe?" he raised an eyebrow at Tamsin who laughed.

"Give Robin my love. Now that's a case of all's well that ends well!" She turned to Sara and explained, "I worked for Robin when I first came to Malvern. It was kinda my first case, I suppose you could say. Where it all began …"

"You'll have to tell me all about it," smiled Sara, "but right now I have news."

Feargal sat down again. "Be quick and I can hear it too."

"Well, you should have heard the ructions from the office after you left!"

Tamsin glanced at Feargal, who nodded back.

"Brenda surely took Howard apart. Lots of 'This is the last time,' and 'I won't cover for you any more'. I couldn't hear it all, but my goodness, he was definitely put in his place."

"That's just what we expected. Good girl Brenda! Now I really have to rush," and as quick as his word, Feargal was out of the door and striding up the hill, shoulders hunched and woolly-hatted head bent into the cold North wind and the now relentless drizzle.

"Whatever did you do? What kicked all that off?" asked Sara, happily accepting the coffee Kylie had brought over, and giving her her card.

Tamsin filled her in on what had transpired in the shop a short while ago.

"Wow. So I came in and smashed his alibi. Poor Howard."

"Don't know about 'poor Howard' - he's brought it all on himself. He's certainly made himself an object of pity, the way he's carrying on."

"But, you know, I don't see him as a murderer, I really don't. I don't think he has the bottle."

"I tend to agree with you. Although, as you saw in Bishop's Green, murderers can come in surprising guises!"

"True. And just like then, all that business with the bows and arrows - you had to work out who was really involved and who was a distraction, an also-ran? I think that's what you have to do now. There's so much smoke and mirrors here, obscuring the truth."

"A shaft of Emerald-like brilliance, if I may say so!" laughed Tamsin. "It does seem that everyone in this sorry affair has something to hide. And it's a question of whether they're the main menu or a side dish."

"Nice way of putting it! Where is Emerald, by the way? I haven't seen her since the the bike race in the Forest.

"She's doing one of her meditation retreats today. It's what fills her up. I'm glad. The shed business was quite a shock for her."

"Poor Emerald. Mark told me all about that crazy business! Give her my love - I'll see her on Tuesday for class. I have a couple of days off - staff training or something at college. Don't have to get in till Wednesday." She sipped her drink. "Andrew says there's a lot of ill-feeling in the Nighthawks. They're losing their trust in each other because of the sabotage attempts, and then there's this unresolved murder hanging over them ..."

"Does Andrew go up there a lot?"

"Not every week. He has squash some nights, then in the summer he does rock-climbing .."

"He's a very athletic type, is your Andrew."

Sara blushed to her roots. "I don't know about 'my Andrew'."

"Sorry, not meaning anything. He's a nice guy. Perhaps he'd be wise to play a bit more squash for now?"

"I've already said that, especially after all that business in the Forest last week. I'll tell him you said it - he may listen then," they laughed together then she paused, drawing a circle in the spilt water on the table-top. "I'm wondering if I'm safe at the shop now, what with Howard going off his trolley and kidnapping you."

"I think Brenda should have him in hand. But you shouldn't feel afraid to go to work. Why not talk to Brenda and explain how you feel? She won't want to lose you - she does like your work, doesn't she?"

"She says she does, and I have to say I do enjoy it there. Working Saturdays and having access to these nice shops works well for me. Especially during term-time when Crystal is at College all the time."

"Gottit," murmured Tamsin.

"There was a time when I overheard Howard telling Brenda he wanted to give some work to Majella - you know, the speedy cyclist?"

"Really? Well, I'm sure Brenda will knock that on the head now! Let's hope she really wields the rolling pin good-o. Time her errant husband was brought in line. He's been teetering on the illegal ..."

"Oh, look at the time - I must fly! I want to catch that woo-woo shop before I go back to work. I'd like one of their fairy pendants."

"That would suit you well, with your elfin face! I must get going too - got some accounts to get done. Sadly, they don't do themselves!" She stood and wound her scarf round her face and pulled on her gloves. "Be sure to buttonhole Brenda when she's on her own. Make her realise what else she could lose."

CHAPTER TWENTY-SEVEN

Tamsin spent some of the afternoon and evening doing her accounts for the month, interspersed with dog games and dog walks. Her tolerance for fiddling about with numbers scribbled on scraps of paper was low, and breaks were frequent and necessary to keep her sane.

She was working on a new trick with Banjo and Quiz together. They started by sitting in front of her then hopped up and walked backwards very fast for a few yards, before ending with a sweeping bow, front legs flat on the ground and tails waving in the air. And she was playing this with them on Sunday morning when Emerald appeared.

"That looks like the end of a tricks display," said Emerald, yawning as she came down the stairs, her long blonde hair tangled and slept in. And there was the dot-dot-dot of Opal padding down the stairs beside her.

"It's just a bit of fun - tying a few of their tricks together into a sequence. It's 'Go back' which they know means run backwards away from me, and 'Take a bow' which is the bow bit. No purpose really, except to spare me from accounts for a few minutes yesterday," she laughed.

"Hate accounts," muttered Emerald as she pointed to the kettle and raised her eyebrows questioningly.

"Absolutely, yes please! Have you ever heard me say no to coffee?"

Tamsin said, "Hey, the light's flashing on my phone - I did all my calls last night. Do you think ...?" and she leapt forward to check it, looking meaningfully at Emerald, who paused to listen.

She chucked the phone down. "No message, hidden number," she said to Emerald. "This is beginning to annoy me."

"Nothing we can do right now - let's eat." For once Emerald was being more practical than her housemate.

And they made themselves comfortable in the living room in front of the gas fire to enjoy their breakfast together.

"What news from the battlefront?" asked Emerald after a while, her long green skirt draped over her legs which were tucked up beneath her on the sofa, Opal's cream fur making a wonderful contrast with the rich deep green as she reposed on her lap, eyes closed, purring blissfully.

"Sure you want to know?"

"Yes, I'm fine now thanks. Got it all resolved during my meditation session yesterday, and a couple of releasing yoga practices."

"You're lucky you have an escape mechanism!"

"I knew I couldn't just keep hiding from it. I had to face it, how I felt, what happened. Only then could I put it in its place. I didn't want to be haunted by it forever."

Tamsin reached over and pressed her friend's arm. "You have a wise head on those shapely shoulders, Emerald. Well, this is what we've found out ..." and she detailed what they had discovered since the shed incident.

"So Jim has his hand in the till," Emerald summed up, "Howard is soft on Majella bordering on the obsessional, both have been telling lies all over the place, we still don't know who's doing the sabotaging or why, we don't know where Johnny Lightholder fits into all this, we don't know the full connection between Majella and Ambrose, and we absolutely have no idea who killed Ferdinand."

"Got it. In one," said Tamsin glumly, reaching for the muzzle that had appeared on her lap in sympathy, and stroking Quiz's eyebrows.

"I think that Majella is not as squeaky-clean as she'd like us all to think. Howard's actions may have been inappropriate, but she's clearly been encouraging him."

"Feargal was suggesting we ought to talk to her again. I think you're right. She's certainly linked to the two guys from Shropshire. And it must have been Ferdinand's questions about Ambrose that wound Howard up."

"Presumably she was living with him?"

"Seems most likely. And he must have left her when the firm went bust and he disappeared with the money."

"The money Ferdinand was trying to trace."

"She's got to know more than she's letting on. I'm thinking .." Emerald lifted Opal up off her lap while she adjusted her legs under her, "I'm thinking she may be the key to the whole thing."

"You think Majella murdered Ferdinand?" Tamsin asked quickly.

"I wouldn't go that far. But I do think she knows." Opal settled down again and resumed purring.

"They do good things ... they all teach the kids' bike classes on the Common. Ooh! I'm sure Molly said it was on Sundays. I wonder …"

"Great idea! But I think we should have Feargal there too. He knows about the company as he's been investigating it, didn't you say?"

"Good plan. Let's give him a ring. Hey, can you see if you can find any mention of the bike classes?" and they both bent over their phones.

Emerald did find, and Tamsin connected with Feargal, so they all aimed to wander innocently across the Common with dogs towards the end of the training session, just before it got dark.

They just needed to find the one thing that held all this together. Perhaps this time they'd really find out what was going on.

CHAPTER TWENTY-EIGHT

"There they are!" Feargal pointed excitedly down the hill at the crowd of children of all ages, some wobbling about on their bikes, and some doing clever stuff on them, weaving round plastic cones and seeing how long they could balance upright with both feet off the ground.

"I can see Adam .."

"There's Cynthia!"

"I guess Django is off nursing his injured arm - wait a minute - there's Majella, over by that silver birch." Tamsin called the dogs in and put them on lead so they could get closer without disrupting the class.

But her hopes were dashed as soon as Cameron and his brothers saw them all. There was a screech of delight and little Joe cast his bike down on the spot and ran to them. Cameron and the middle boy, Alex, took the opportunity to show off their skills, and carried on weaving through the cones. They soon found that waving with one hand, leaving only one hand on the handlebars, made balancing (and showing off) harder, so they cycled over to join Joe and greet the dogs, with their usual level of excitement.

"Hey boys! You'll get us in trouble for spoiling your class!" Tamsin laughed, as the dogs happily waved their tails while the boys chattered, all trying to talk at the same time about how they were the best at cycling.

"I like your helmets," said Emerald in an excess of parent-like care, "you look so cool!"

"Mine has Superbiker on it!" Joe pointed to the cartoon image on the front of his helmet.

"Are you looking for Mum?" asked Alex, hopping from foot to foot as ever.

"Just taking the afternoon air," Feargal lied easily. "I've been trying out this mountain biking lark, up on the Hills."

"Coo!" the three boys gazed at him with saucer eyes.

"At night?" asked Cameron.

"Yep, at night. Have to have good lights." Cameron gaped at Feargal in admiration. "It's hard, I can tell you. And painful!" he grinned. "Oh, isn't that some of the Nighthawks over there?"

Joe pushed in front of his bigger brothers, "Yes, the Nighthawks teach us!"

"Well, I think you'd better get back to what you were doing. They're looking over here."

"Race you!" cried Alex, grabbing his bike from the ground, and the three boys whizzed back to the course, little Joe shouting in frustration as they pulled ahead, running after them to reach where he'd left his bike.

"Let's wander about till the class is over," Tamsin released the dogs as they moved up the hill where they spent a pleasant ten minutes playing fetch with Banjo's frisbee. Feargal could throw it further than either Tamsin or Emerald, so Banjo quickly learnt just who to take the toy to every time he caught it.

"They learn fast," laughed Feargal, as he danced forward for a massive throw.

Eventually the tired children started to wind their way up the hill with their bikes to get to the car park and their parents' cars. Alex and Cynthia were packing up the plastic cones and a few other poles and markers, while Majella chatted to a man and his small daughter who was wanting to book on to sessions.

"Heading back to the car, Majella!" called Alex, the big box of cones on his hip, Cynthia carrying the poles.

"Ok, I'm on two wheels, so I'll see you on Wednesday," she called back, as the man and child turned to leave.

"This is our moment," whispered Tamsin, and they walked towards Majella, spreading out slightly. As they reached her, Tamsin told the two big dogs to lie down, while Moonbeam hopped up into her arms.

"You again?" she said rather rudely. "I've told you all I know."

"I don't think so," said Tamsin.

"You haven't mentioned that you were living with Ambrose for a couple of years .." Feargal put in, watching Majella give him a startled look.

"Or that he was in business with Ferdinand .." added Tamsin.

"Or that when he left you he left with the cash from the business." Emerald folded her arms.

Majella dropped her cocky look for a moment and said, "I don't know how you know, but yes, that's about it. I was a fool. I was bowled over by the handsome suave Ambrose, and I trusted him. And Ferdinand." She kicked a tussock of grass with her foot.

"So you were not best pleased when Ferdinand showed up in your life again?"

"Too right I wasn't. I wanted to be free of both of them."

"So where's Ambrose now?" Feargal asked.

"Who knows? He took quite a lot of money, I think, which was what Ferdinand was after. He must have thought I was still in touch with his one-time partner."

"So did you help Ferdinand?"

"No way! I wanted nothing to do with either of them ever again. You see," she leaned back against the silver birch, "Ferdinand was a mountain biker. I met him at a bike event in Shropshire. It was he who introduced me to Ambrose, curse him. It was all his fault!" Majella's voice was rising, she was gesticulating with her arms and her cheeks were blazing red. "If only he'd stayed away .." then she stopped herself abruptly.

"'If only he'd stayed away ..' what, Majella? What would have happened?" asked Tamsin.

"Or rather," said Feargal quietly, "what *wouldn't* have happened?"

Majella suddenly looked just like Howard - a trapped animal. She turned and started to run towards her bike over by the hedge. Feargal, standing a little to one side, was wrong-footed and slow to move, so Tamsin yelled "GO BACK!" and Quiz and Banjo both jumped up and started to race backwards between the running Majella and her bike. She was about to run right past them when Tamsin called out "TAKE A BOW!" and both dogs dropped their front legs flat on the ground, tails waving in the air with excitement, and Majella fell right over them.

They all ran up to her, Feargal standing ready to grab her if she moved again, and Emerald bending down to her and asking her if she was ok. Tamsin's priority was to check her beloved dogs, who fortunately had suffered no ill effects and were happy to receive little pieces of sausage for their part in the "citizen's arrest".

"Will you never leave me alone?!" Majella squawked. "What has this to do with you?"

"Remember it was Emerald and I who happened on the unfortunate Ferdinand shortly after he died. I think you owe us an explanation."

"You won't believe me," she moaned as she dropped her head in her hands, still sitting on the ground.

"Try us." Feargal said through gritted teeth.

"It's going to come out eventually," Emerald said, now sitting beside her, "you can't keep a secret like this for ever."

Tamsin turned to glance at Emerald and mouthed silently, "What do you know?"

"I can see what happened," said Emerald, with a faraway look in her eye. "And we do understand, Majella, we really do!"

Majella looked up with a stricken expression. "You're right. I can't keep running away. I suppose this is the end of the road. I may as well tell you." She took a deep breath. "I'd heard Ferdinand was asking around for Ambrose."

"Howard?"

Majella nodded. "He knew that pair had been bad news for me, so he warned me off. Then Ferdinand appeared on the Hills on New Year's Eve. I'd seen him there and pulled my visor down and kept well away from him. It was just after the fireworks. The others had all gone up to the North Hill to avoid the crowds, but I'd dropped one of my lights and came back to look for it. I saw it flickering on the ground and was about to mount up and ride away with it when I spotted the glint of metal in the moonlight. There was Ferdinand, lying next to his upturned bike. There was a walking pole caught in his front wheel. Someone must have dropped it in the crowd of people leaving, and he got tangled up in it and crashed and broke his lights. Maybe he hit a rock when he fell - his neck was at a funny angle." Tamsin nodded, her face grim, clearly remembering. Majella kneaded the hem of her jacket with shaking fingers. "I thought he was dead." She gazed into the middle distance as she went on, very quietly. "I felt a surge of hatred for him, for having landed me in so much trouble. I snatched the walking pole from his wheel and I ... I pointed it at his chest ... I thought he was already dead!" Her voice was becoming a shriek. "Really, I did!"

"And you leant on it ...?" Tamsin felt sick.

Majella put her head back in her hands. "I said 'You broke my heart so I'm going to break yours!' I leant on it. And I left."

There was a stunned silence.

"I thought he was already dead!" she cried, tears now flowing down her red cheeks. "And when they said he'd died of being stabbed I was shocked. I didn't know what to do! I didn't think anyone had seen me, so I just kept quiet."

"What did you do with the pole?" asked the ever-practical Feargal.

"I realised I was still holding it when I was cycling up the hill. I'd run away so fast. When I reached the edge of one of the flooded quarries I chucked it over."

"And you hoped it would all disappear, like the pole in the lake?" Emerald said soothingly, her hand on the desperate girl's arm. "The only way it will go away is if you face it. I know this."

"You can't run for the rest of your life," Tamsin said.

And Feargal added reassuringly, "They'll take all your story into account. They won't lock you up and throw away the key, really they won't."

Majella pushed on the ground. "I .. I can't move." She looked white and panicked. Emerald wrapped her scarf round the girl's shaking shoulders.

"Shock," said Tamsin firmly. "Let's call an ambulance."

Feargal nodded as he spoke into the phone at his ear. "Yes please, ambulance and police. Both."

CHAPTER TWENTY-NINE

"Mmmm, this cake is delicious!" said Tamsin, licking the last of it from her spoon.

"The Furies have excelled themselves. What do they call this one?" said Sara.

"Coffee and Hazelnut Gateau, I believe," said Emerald, half her cake still to be eaten.

"It's such a relief to be sitting here without worrying," added Sara. "*Flying Pedals* is so much calmer. It's only six weeks since Howard started his counselling, but it's all much less frantic."

"Is Brenda running the show now?"

"Yep. She's taken over officially. She's now the Managing Director, and Howard has an advisory role. Even Jason is more forthcoming and friendly."

Emerald waved her spoon in the air, "He was probably forever put down by his father."

"You're right, I think. Brenda's preparing him for a bigger part in the business than just being a mechanic in the workshop." She put her fork on her plate and looked at its emptiness wistfully for a moment. "Jason and Mark seem to be working together nicely. Mark's thinking of joining us permanently."

"Oh yes, he must be nearly through his training course." Tamsin looked longingly at Emerald's half-eaten cake, took a firm hold on herself and added, "bet Shirley's proud of him."

"At last!" laughed Emerald. "She's had to wait a long time. That's devotion for you. Ah, here's Feargal! He said he'd be dropping by." Kylie waved to him from the counter with a thumbs-up so he came straight over to the table.

"Hey everyone! Tamsin," he turned to her as he reached for a chair, "before I forget - the boss wants you to explain that trick in your next diary post. The one with the dogs going backwards."

"Oh, ok. It's not a beginner trick, but I'll see what I can do."

"He's pleased with your articles, and he likes the way you deal with the mailbag too. Your personal answers in the paper encourage reader participation - I think that's the buzzword."

Tamsin gloated. *Fancy being a published writer!* she thought to herself. And as Kylie brought over Feargal's coffee they all shuffled their chairs round, carefully avoiding the dogs on their mats, to make space for him. "Tell you what, Feargal - I'll have plenty more to write about soon: I'm starting training with the Search and Rescue guys next week."

"Orange jacket for Banjo?" he asked.

"Definitely! You'll look lovely, so you will, Banjo Bunny!"

"Get that chair over too, Feargal," said Emerald, "Look who's coming in!"

"Charity!" chorused Tamsin and Feargal. "Come and join us. Haven't seen you for ages. You been down to Torquay to visit your grand-niece again?"

"Yes I have. Poor Sophie sprained her ankle, so it was the least I could do to go back down and help." She leant over conspiratorially and grinned, "and a great excuse to see the baby again and enjoy watching the winter storms over the sea. Muffin does love the beach!"

There was much tail-wagging as Muffin greeted her old friend Moonbeam and they lay down on Moonbeam's mat together.

"So," declared Charity. "I see from the *Malvern Mercury* that that whole Glossop murder is done and dusted. You *have* to tell me all about it!" She leant back and folded her arms across her chest, only to reach out straight away to field the mug of tea that Kylie had brought her. As she reached for her purse, Feargal said "I'll get these, Kylie," and put his card on her tray. Charity smiled sweetly at him and nodded her thanks.

"Well, you heard that Majella O'Donovan was arrested for the murder?" Tamsin began.

"Yes, so sad. Her family must be devastated."

"There are mitigating circumstances. The charge may be lessened," Feargal said.

"I do hope so. She seems to have got caught up in a lot of other people's ambitions. We'll just have to wait for the trial, I suppose. But how did you know, dear?"

"We had a load of loose ends. Lots of circumstantial evidence and no certainty. We narrowed it down to being an inside job - that the Nighthawks were involved, not a random stranger. And with some investigative stuff from Feargal we learned of the tie-up with Howard, Majella, and Ambrose. We wanted to talk to Majella again, to establish the truth of the relationship, and Emerald came out with one of her shafts of insight," she nodded to Emerald who blushed a pretty pale pink, "and the poor girl just broke down and confessed."

There was a moment's silence for the unfortunate Majella.

"And if my mystery caller had got brave enough to talk to me earlier, we'd have all got there a lot sooner," said Tamsin.

"Mystery caller?" asked Sara.

"I kept getting silent calls. No number. And as soon as they heard my message and that I wasn't in they'd ring off. I don't normally answer calls in the day - I do them all in the evening, when I've got my booking sheet and calendar all ready. But, eventually, they rang when I was there. And as soon as I saw 'number withheld' I grabbed the phone and answered!"

"So who was it?" Sara was agog.

"Turns out to be some weirdo photographer. He was at the fireworks then decided to wander up the hill after. 'The blue light on the snow was so beautiful,' he said. And when he examined his photos a couple of days later, he saw that he'd caught a cyclist in the act of tossing something into the quarry."

"Wow!" said Sara and Charity together.

"He wanted to give me the photo. So, of course I said, why not give it to the police? And why do you keep ringing and never leaving a message? Know what he said? 'I know you've got a tie-up with the local paper. I've been wanting to get my pictures in there for ages - be a roving photographer for them.'"

"You're kidding! He had evidence in a murder enquiry and he held on to it all this time?" Sara was aghast. "He must be nuts!"

"Honestly, he did sound nuts. I needed to get that photo, so I arranged for him to leave it at the *Malvern Mercury* front desk with my name on, saying I'd get it to my contacts there. Which I kinda did. Feargal picked it up, and sure enough, it's clearly Majella throwing the walking pole into the lake."

"What are you going to do with it, dear?" asked Charity. "The picture I mean."

"Oh, Feargal dropped it over to Hawkins. We don't either of us want to have anything to do with that nutcase, and I expect by the time Hawkins has finished tearing him off a strip he'll be looking for a new hobby!"

"So where did she get the pole from?" asked Sara.

Feargal knew the answer to this one, "Someone left their walking pole leaning against the hedge during the fireworks display, and Ferdinand's front wheel caught it. That's what catapulted him off his bike. Nobody would have heard, what with all the noise from the fireworks. Then the pole's owner rang to report it stolen a couple of days later. But no-one in the station made the connection."

"I suppose the people on the desk didn't know what Tamsin had discovered?"

"No. Not their fault - just a bit of miscommunication. Anyway, it wouldn't have been much help as it was already at the bottom of the lake.

Only once Majella had confessed to throwing it in were they able to send divers down to retrieve it."

"And it matched?"

"Yep. Conclusive evidence. Exactly matched the marks on the body."

They all paused to drink their coffees in silence. Then Charity lifted the mood. "And what about that buffoon Jim Hansom? Didn't you think he was tied up in it somehow?"

"Turns out he had his hand in the Nighthawks' till. He'd been doing some shady dealings on the stock exchange and the bills had come home to roost," Feargal explained.

"And another wife came to the rescue?" Sara piped up.

Tamsin looked up from stroking Quiz's head, "Gillian has her own money. So he had to confess to her and she bailed him out. I think he'll be on a short lead from now on!"

"Oh my. And what about that Howard fellow?"

"He simply refuses to explain what he was doing at the shop when he says he was doing the accounts - "

"- but he wasn't," put in Sara.

"I suspect it was nothing more pernicious than watching lycra-clad women mountain bikers on video. And, honestly, I don't think we want to know. Brenda knows, and assures us it's nothing criminal. But she has him well in hand, and apparently he's on his best behaviour now."

Sara added, "He's getting help for his obsessions. And he's much less fiery and bossy already. I have to say, he's never done anything bad to me. You know, from that point of view ..." she blushed and reached to stroke Quiz's head to distract herself.

"These errant husbands ..." sighed Charity. "Then you said there were people causing accidents - that threw you to begin with, didn't it? You thought that's what may have happened to Ferdinand?"

"Quite so," agreed Tamsin. "Such a coincidence. Well there are more men behaving badly there. Some of the tough-looking guys we met at the memorial had formed a betting ring. They stood to do quite nicely if the Nighthawks stars didn't do well in the World competitions. They've been uncovered by the police and naturally have been thrown out of the group."

"Thrown out of cycling altogether, I believe. Blacklisted," nodded Feargal.

"Disgraceful behaviour!" said Charity indignantly.

"They're awaiting trial now, too."

"And did anyone ever track down the elusive Ambrose, at the bottom of all this trouble?" asked Charity, ever seeking justice and right.

"Nope. Guess he's living in Spain or South America or somewhere on the money he stole."

"I wonder if he reads the English papers?" mused Emerald.

"If he does, he'd do well to keep his head down till this all passes over, so he can continue to enjoy his ill-gotten gains," Feargal said, folding his arms firmly to show his opinion of Ambrose.

Sara sipped her coffee and said, "But the good news is that Django's arm is healing well and he'll be able to do the remaining qualifier. And he seems to have got over his interest in Majella pretty fast. I understand he's training with Sally now, the other up-and-coming Nighthawk," she raised an eyebrow and grinned.

"Adam and Cynthia, Django and Sally, Andrew and ...?" Feargal teased Sara, who wriggled uncomfortably. "He's focussing on rock-climbing now," she pouted, then grinned.

"Oh!" Tamsin clapped her hands together with delight and they all turned to her to listen. "And I got to the bottom of the secret package passed to Johnny Lightholder at the memorial. You see I ran into him last week at the supermarket - in the haircare aisle," she nodded knowingly. "I asked him straight out - what was the secret package? He looked cringingly embarrassed, lifted his woolly hat up and pointed to his temple. 'Losing my hair', he said quietly, glancing around to see we weren't being overheard. Seems it was a treatment the others had picked up abroad on a cycling trip. Not approved here. 'Look,' he whined at me, 'you won't tell anyone, will you?'" They all laughed uproariously, happy to have something light to laugh about, rocking back and forward in their seats.

"So now you've told us!" said Emerald, open-mouthed.

"I said to him that I wouldn't tell any of his fellow riders. You're all different. You're part of the investigation!" They laughed again, "and that includes you crowd down there on the floor," she said reaching into her pocket for some treats for Quiz, Banjo, Moonbeam and Muffin. You're the stars of the show, after all!" Then she asked them to get up and said, "Take a bow!" at which all three of hers took a bow, while Muffin, not to be left out, lay down with her chin on her paws.

Charity smiled, "Looks like 'Tamsin the Malvern Detective' will have to be re-named 'The Malvern Dog Detectives'!"

Want to read the other books in this popular series? You'll find them here:

https://mybook.to/TamsinKernickCozies

^^^ Scan the code above or click here

To find out how Tamsin arrived in Malvern and began Top Dogs, you can read this free novella "Where it all began" at

https://urlgeni.us/Lucyemblemcozy

and we'll be able to let you know when Tamsin's next adventure is ready for you!

And if you enjoyed this book, I'd love it if you could whiz over to where you bought it and leave a brief review, so others may find it and enjoy it as well, and be kind to their animals!

ALL THE TAMSIN KERNICK COZY ENGLISH MYSTERIES

Where it all began ..

https://urlgeni.us/Lucyemblemcozy

Sit, Stay, Murder!

https://mybook.to/SitStayMurder

Ready, Aim, Woof!

https://mybook.to/ReadyAimWoof

Down Dog!

https://mybook.to/TamsinKernickCozies

Barks, Bikes, and Bodies!

https://mybook.to/TamsinKernickCozies

ABOUT THE AUTHOR

From an early age I loved animals. From doing "showjumping" in the back garden with Simon, the long-suffering family pet - many years before Dog Agility was invented - I worked in the creative arts till I came back to my first love and qualified as a dog trainer.

Working for years with thousands of dogs and their colourful owners - from every walk of life - I found that their fancies and foibles, their doings and their undoings, served to inspire this series of cozy mysteries.

While the varying characters weave their way through the books, some becoming established personnel in the stories, the stars of the show are the animals!

They don't have human powers. They don't need to. They have plenty of powers of their own, which need only patience and kindness to bring out and enjoy with them.

If you enjoyed this story, I would LOVE it if you could hop over to where you purchased your book and leave a brief review!

Lucy Emblem

facebook.com/lucyemblemcozies

Printed by BoD"in Norderstedt, Germany